"How has this
"You're kiddin̶̶̶̶̶̶̶̶̶̶̶̶̶̶̶̶̶̶̶̶̶̶̶̶̶̶̶̶̶̶̶ ̶̶̶̶̶̶phone videos?
It was probably on TMZ before the coroner even got to the lot. MJ ran into Ryder's arms when he appeared at the door. I'm happy he's here for her."

A tear ran down her cheek. He wiped it away with his thumb. "Aw, don't cry, Ames. I'm here for you. I'll get to the bottom of all this."

"Why Mike? Why would anyone want to hurt MJ?"

"I don't know, but I'll find out. I contacted your dad requesting involvement in the case. He must have talked with Flynn who has a history working with the LAPD. Small world, Flynn knows the lead detective. I'm on the investigative team officially. I have a meeting with the lead detective first thing in the morning."

"MJ said she wants to resume shooting tomorrow if the police let her. I'll have an early start to the day, too."

"I don't see any reason why you can't go back to work – if MJ adds a heavy security presence. I'll talk to her before I leave for my meeting in the morning. She needs to close the set and post guards at all studio access points. I'm still concerned about her exposure."

"I know. I'm sure she'll listen to you."

He huffed a laugh. "Have you met my sister?"

Mike stroked Amy's silken hair. "Get some sleep, sweetheart. I'll keep you safe."

Praise

"Watch out...the Sullivan Boys are a force to be reckoned with!" National Bestselling Author Brenda Novak

Against Doctors Orders: "This story has it all." Got Erotic Romance Reviews

Beyond the Code of Conduct: "Plenty of big-Irish-family passion. lush descriptions and lots of emotion...from its exciting beginning to its unexpected ending." Between the Lines Book Reviews (Fantastic)

Capturing Karma: "Fantastic read!" Night Owl Reviews

All's Fair in Love and Law: "In one word, this book is awesome." The Book Connection

In The St. Nick of Time: "Fantastic...a keeper." RT Book Reviews

Sullivan Boys Award Winning Series: New England Bean Pot Readers Choice, The Lories, Borders Books Readers Crown Finalist, Book Connection #6 Top Ten Books 2009, #4 Romantic Suspense books

From the First Moment

by

K. M. Daughters

Love!

Sequel to the Sullivan Boys Series

K. M. Daughters

This is a work of fiction. Names, characters, places, and incidents are either the product of the author's imagination or are used fictitiously, and any resemblance to actual persons living or dead, business establishments, events, or locales, is entirely coincidental.

From the First Moment

Cover Art by *Kim Mendoza*

The Wild Rose Press, Inc.
PO Box 708
Adams Basin, NY 14410-0708
Visit us at www.thewildrosepress.com

Publishing History
First Edition, 2023
Trade Paperback ISBN
Digital ISBN

Sequel to the Sullivan Boys Series
Published in the United States of America

Dedication

For Patti. You are the Storm.

Acknowledgments

A heart full of gratitude for the angels at Northwestern Memorial, for prayers offered on shooting stars and for all those who held K.M. Daughters in their hearts during this writing. Because of you our storytelling will go on…hopefully for a long, long time.

Thank you, Ally Robertson, for the joyful work of editing another book with you. As always, your talent and your expert guidance are invaluable. You are a treasured friend and a blessing.

Thank you to our first fairy God-Editors, Joelle Walker, and Nicola Martinez. Fifteen years ago, as of January 26, 2023, you made our dream of becoming published authors come true and we will always be grateful – for your good taste. ☺

Thank you to The Wild Rose Press and Pelican Book Group, publishers of the year.

Thank you to our cheerleading, beautiful families for your love, your encouragement and for reading and listening to our books and audiobooks.

And to you, dear Reader. Thank you for spending time with Amy and Mike. We hope you loved their story.

Other Wild Rose Press Titles by K. M. Daughters:

Against Doctors Orders
All's Fair in Love and Law
Bewitching Breeze
Beyond the Code of Conduct
Capturing Karma
Fill the Stadium
From the First Moment
In the St. Nick of Time
Only One Summer
Reunion for the First Time
Skye Without Limits
The Sullivan Boys

Chapter 1

Amy Jordan Sullivan touched up her lipstick peering into the dressing room mirror at the Chicago Theatre. She tucked an escaped strand of long raven hair under her blonde shoulder-length wig, and then bent at the waist to slip her feet into white sneakers. Amy completed her transformation draping the white cardigan that hung on the back of her chair around her shoulders. Innocent, pure Sandy gazed back at Amy in the mirror.

When Amy was offered the role in the Chicago Theater limited engagement of her favorite musical, *Grease*, she jumped at the chance. Not only was she eager to play a lead character but also, the weeks-long run would allow her to spend time with her family, especially her mom. She and her mother had developed a special bond after her father was killed in off duty action during a liquor store robbery when Amy was ten years old. Although those difficult years as the only child of a widowed mom were long behind them, she and her mother, Molly had grown closer into Amy's adulthood.

Amy didn't regret following her dream and moving to California years ago to pursue an acting career. She loved her life and growing professional success, but still sorely missed her family. Even though the luxurious house she now owned in the Hollywood Hills provided plenty of space for visitors, her parents rarely made the trip to the coast more than twice a year.

She wasn't entirely separated from her large, boisterous adoptive family, though. Her cousin MJ's job directing films had brought her to California, too. Amy had offered her a temporary place to stay until she could find something more permanent near the Hollywood movie making mecca. MJ had accepted her offer, moved into the guest house, and had since shared expenses – a perfect arrangement for them.

Amy checked the airline app on her phone, excited to see that MJ's flight had landed at O'Hare. Her cousin had meetings in Chicago about her next project. Like Amy, MJ would also spend time with family and even planned on coming to Amy's matinee the next day.

A knock sounded and then Jenna, the actress playing Frenchy, bounded into the dressing room. "Hey Sandy. Ready to go to the race?"

"Let's go, Frenchy," Amy said on a laugh.

She followed Jenna and halted in the wings waiting for their cues. Amy peeked around the curtain and grinned at the sight of Danny Sullivan, her proud dad, in the audience. He held court in the middle of the front row, flanked by his men. He had purchased tickets for the entire front row for every one of her performances and pushed the tickets on family and subordinates on the CPD. She questioned whether the men truly wanted to go to a musical or if they viewed using the tickets as a literal command performance from the Chicago Superintendent of Police.

Jenna finished her lines and left Amy alone on stage. Amy leaned against a tree watching Danny and the T-Birds plan a car race. The lights dimmed and a spotlight bathed her in brilliant white light. When she belted out the last note of the showstopping song, "Look at Me I'm

Sandra Dee," the front row led the audience in a thunderous standing ovation.

She jogged off stage and then broke into a sprint on a bead for the dressing room for her last costume change. Amy stood in place catching her breath as the wardrobe mistress slipped off her cardigan and helped unbutton her shirtwaist dress.

Amy put her hands on Margie's shoulders, stepped out of the dress that had pooled on the floor and plopped down on her dressing table chair. "Thanks, Margie."

Amy slipped off her wig and faced Ellen, the makeup artist who outlined her eyes with black liner with a couple of deft flicks, dabbed her lashes with a heavy mascara and added scarlet red lipstick to complete the vixen, sexy Sandy look.

Bending one leg after the other, Amy circled a bright red tube top over her ankles, stretched it up to her knees and then stood up tugging and wiggling the material up over her hips and then her breasts. Next came the contortions putting on her skintight black pants. Amy held her breath and sucked in her stomach as Margie yanked the zipper all the way up. There was a knock on the door as Amy shimmied into a black leather jacket.

"Come in," she called out.

"Hello beautiful." Ryder Scott, a.k.a. Danny Zuko, strode into the room and bussed Amy's cheek. He held her hand for balance as she slipped into her sky-high heels.

"Perfect timing, Ry, thanks."

He kissed each of her knuckles before letting go of her hand.

Each time Ryder took the stage, women in the audience heaved audible sighs, and they waited by the

3

stage door after each performance hoping for a glimpse of him. He treated his swooning fans with unfailing kindness and stayed however long to provide every autograph and photo. His courtesy surrounding his celebrity had always impressed Amy and served as an example of the best way to appreciate fame.

She had met Ry when she did a guest spot on his immensely popular TV show, *Doctor By Day*. He played the lead, Dr. Waverly, who had a secret life as a rock star musician at night. Amy played his love interest for a few episodes, but sadly her character died despite all of Dr. Waverly's efforts to save the love of his life. Amy didn't win her nominated Emmy for the cameo performance, but Ryder had won his second, Best Actor award that year. They had become fast friends and dated casually for a while. But their relationship stalled in the forever-friends category – at least from Amy's perspective.

"Do you want to grab dinner tonight after the show?" Ry said.

"I'm not sure." Amy gazed at his reflection in her mirror as she pinned up her long hair, and then tugged on a curly blonde wig.

He was drop dead gorgeous, but the most attractive thing about him was his total lack of conceit. Amy was very attracted to Ryder. What woman wouldn't be? But the man who haunted her dreams prevented her from returning his advances.

"Why? Do you have a hot date or something?" He unleashed a dazzling smile meant to convince her of the no contest between him and any other "hot" dates.

"Nope," she said. "I might have a date with my cousin. Her flight just landed at O'Hare. I'm not sure if she wants to have dinner with me tonight or if she would rather just go to her mom's."

"No problem one way or the other. She can join us. I want to meet this cousin. Or is it BFF? Or is it sister that you talk so much about?"

"I do refer to her as all those things, don't I? Sounds a bit scattered when I hear you say it. When I was the new girl in school after moving from New York to Chicago, MJ and I were instant friends. My mom met her uncle Danny when he was brought to her ER with a gunshot wound…"

"Wait. Isn't Danny your dad's name?"

Amy chuckled. "I'm getting to that. Mom and MJ's Uncle Danny started dating and MJ and I were together even more often. Mom married Danny – who yes, is my dad. He adopted me immediately after the wedding. Then MJ officially became my cousin. People called us sisters with different mothers and fathers. If I had to pick one, I guess I would call her my sister, but I understand if I've confused you."

She huffed in amusement. "I think I just confused myself."

"I'm not confused at all. I'd love your sister to join us for dinner."

"I *am* hungry. What do you have in mind?"

"Pizza at Malnati's." He grinned impishly at her frown. "Just kidding. Of course, Bob's Burgers. You love their fries."

"You know me so well. It's a deal if we order the onion rings tower."

"Sweetheart, you can order anything you want." Ry gave her a hug from behind beaming into the mirror at her.

A stagehand rapped on the door. "Two minutes,

guys."

Ry extended his hand. "Now I can't wait until the curtain drops. My stomach is rumbling."

She took his hand and strolled with him out of the dressing room. He left her in the wings on her side of the stage and jogged to his spot on the opposite side.

Surrounded by the Pink Ladies, Amy made her entrance to booming applause. Her metamorphosis from demure to bombshell: the girl who could win Danny Zuko's heart, brought gasps and a couple wolf whistles from the audience.

The audience loudly applauded again when Ryder, sporting a letterman sweater, made his entrance with the T-Birds.

It was theatre magic when Sandy and Danny met center stage and broke into the familiar song, *You're The One That I Want*. Amy was lost in the song and in Ry's eyes. She didn't face the audience until the last refrain. Staring beyond the footlights she gasped softly and stiffened within Ryder's embrace.

"What's wrong?" he whispered in her ear.

"The front row is empty."

Something terrible must have happened in Chicago for Danny and all his men to leave before the final curtain call.

The cast filed out of the wings from both sides of the stage chorusing the finale song, *We Go Together*. Amy sang along, grabbed Ryder's hand, and blended in with the T-Birds and the Pink Ladies. The audience joined in the party atmosphere clapping, gyrating, and singing along with the catchy song. Amy usually loved this part of the performance, but today she felt queasy. Her dad's sudden exit scared her.

After a record five curtain calls, Amy was finally free to run to her dressing room. Her phone was vibrating when she grabbed it, but she missed the call. She had a slew of missed calls.

"Oh no," Amy said as Margie came into the room to help remove her costume.

Margie knit her brow. "Is everything all right?"

Amy shook her head in response and scrolled the list of missed calls. "This can't be good. My mom has called four times and my dad twice since I went onstage for the finale number."

Marge pushed the chair over to Amy and gently pushed her into the seat. "Sit. Take a breath and call your mom back."

Amy called her mother, Molly and was sent to voice mail. She dialed Dad.

He answered on the first ring. "Hi honey."

"Dad, what's going on? I have a bunch of missed calls from you and Mom. Why didn't either of you leave a message?"

"We didn't want to leave this news on your voice mail…" he paused. "Your Aunt Kay was shot."

"What? Oh no!" Amy screeched and tears filled her eyes. "What happened? Is she OK?"

"I'm so sorry, honey. I don't know. I just got to the hospital. She's in surgery and your mom is in the operating room, too. Molly said she would keep us updated."

"Is MJ there?"

"She's on her way and Mike went to get the twins. They should be here soon."

"I'm coming, Dad. MJ will need me." *And maybe Mike.*

"I'll send a squad car to the theatre."

"Thanks, but it will be easier for me to just call an Uber. I'll be there as soon as I can. Please Dad, call me if you have any updates."

"I will honey. I love you. Be careful."

"I love you, too."

Amy ended the call, opened her Uber App, and ordered a car. Luckily there was one in the area with an ETA in five minutes.

"I don't have time to change, Margie. I've got to go to the hospital. My aunt was shot, and she's in surgery now."

Ry knocked on the open door. "Sorry for eavesdropping, but who's in surgery?"

"My Aunt Kay, MJ's mother."

"What do you need? How can I help?"

"Just say a prayer." She grabbed her backpack out of the closet, stuffed a change of clothes and her phone inside, and started for the door.

Ry touched her arm. "I can come with you. I have a car here."

"Thanks." She gave him a hug. "But my Uber will be here any second. I'll be okay."

She dashed out into the hallway and bolted outside through the stage door.

Seated in the compact car, she checked her phone with shaking hands. "Hopefully no news is good news," she mumbled.

The car tires screeched as the driver accelerated to merge into city traffic.

Chapter 2

"Chicago Regional Hospital, please."

The driver's round brown eyes met hers in the rearview mirror, worry lines crinkled on his face. "Are you unwell? Is this an emergency?"

"No, I'm fine. But a relative is injured and I need to get there as soon as I can."

He shifted his focus straight ahead through the windshield. "Gotcha. This theatre traffic is a bear. I'll take Lower Wacker soon as I can get us out of this snarl."

"Thanks." Amy alternated staring out the window aimlessly and staring at her phone's screen. She gripped the device as if she could wring out an update from her family by sheer force. Preferably, her mom would contact her because that would mean Aunt Kay's surgery had ended.

The car idled at yet another red light. "Uh, miss?"

Amy raised her head and gazed into the review mirror connecting again with the driver's gaze. "Yes?"

"If you don't mind my saying so, my eyes almost popped out of my head when you got into my car. You look sensational." He waggled his brows.

A smile played on Amy's lips despite worrying about Aunt Kay. "Oh. Thanks a lot." She touched the crown of her head. "A wig. I'm playing Sandy in *Grease*."

"Oh, I know, Miss Jordan Sullivan. My wife's a big

fan."

"Of the musical? I don't blame her. I love it, too."

"Well, yes, that, too. But I meant *your* fan. She never misses *Doctor By Day*. Do you believe I came home one night, and she was crying? Because you died. I kept telling her you were alive and well. Even showed her some news about you on the net. Didn't help." He hooted a bawdy har-har.

Amy burst out laughing. She clapped a hand over her mouth. "I shouldn't disrespect the dead."

"You look pretty good for a corpse," he said straight faced, mirth dancing in his eyes.

Amy couldn't squelch another laughing fit. She had company from the front seat. Glad for the silly distraction and his skill maneuvering the car, she realized her ride had almost come to end. The hospital marquee blazed ahead.

"You want the ER Entrance?" he said.

"Yes. That's good."

She opened her purse and took out her wallet. Just short of the entrance, she leaned her forearm over the front seat, cash in hand. "Here's something extra for getting me here so fast."

He waved the money away. "No need…if I could trouble you for an autograph for my wife?"

"Of course. What's her name? And your name, also?"

"She's Debra, but she goes by Debs. And I'm Wayne."

"Nice to meet you, Wayne."

He braked the car, shoved the shift into park and handed her a business card and a pen.

Amy wrote a brief thank you to Debs for her

devotion and signed her name.

Handing the card and pen back to Wayne, she said, "Do you have another one of those cards?"

"Sure."

She accepted the business card and slipped it into her purse. "I'll send some tickets to *Grease* for you and Debs, and some spares, too. Thanks again, Wayne."

Amy opened the door, slipped out of her seat and power walked through the familiar automatic doors. It didn't seem that seven years had passed since Amy had swept through those doors.

"Whoa, look at you," Trudy asserted. "Vavavavoom."

Her mother's favorite Physician's Assistant apparently couldn't resist singing a few bars of "You're The One That I Want," as she hustled out from behind the intake desk, her arms open wide.

The unrestrained hug comforted and uplifted Amy. But, reuniting with Trudy beneath the high-intensity recessed lights of the always over-bright trauma center brought back a rush of memories. Amy vividly remembered how Trudy had acted as her big sister and consoler when she was a kid while her mother, an ER doctor, fought to "put Humpty back together again."

Toddler Amy had interpreted the nursery rhyme as the best description of her mom's job and the Humpty Dumpty metaphor stuck as an inside joke between them through the years. Too often in the past the broken were people that Amy loved: her father; her former nanny, now Aunt Bobbie; her adoptive dad when he met her mother; his brother, Joe; her Aunt Matty; and her Uncle Mike Lynch. Amy bowed her head at the memories. Neither her mom nor any of the other specialists there were able to put Uncle Mike back together again. Now, Mike's widow, Kay, remarried to Uncle Flynn Dowd, lay broken somewhere within these walls.

"Do you have any word on Aunt Kay?"

"Still in surgery last I heard. The waiting room is overrun with men and women in blue right now."

Amy grinned. "Sounds like home. Where do I go?"

"SIT family lounge."

"Third floor and East Wing, right?"

"You got it." Trudy gave her another hug. "I hate the circumstances, but it's so good to see you home. I've missed you."

"I missed you, too. It's good to be back. Catch up with you later?"

"I'd like that."

Amy swung around the intake desk and zipped through the double doors leading to the ER, Molly's domain, to cut through to the elevator bank. Navigating these labyrinthine halls was deeply imbedded in her muscle memory. She had always thought of the huge regional trauma center as her mother's sole territory. Molly had never wanted to practice any other specialty long before she had entered medical school. Her mother had earned the Chief Physician title for this ER, so now, the place could be called Molly's realm officially.

During the elevator ride, Amy's thoughts whirled: worry about Aunt Kay mixed with panic at the inevitable prospect of seeing her aunt's-by-marriage children that day. MJ was a constant in Amy's life. But Kay's son was a very different story.

Her reverie was broken the second the pneumonic doors slid open on the third floor. A swarm of Homicide Division, Lieutenant Kay Dowd's comrades in arms paced the hall and congregated outside the glass doors fronting the sprawling surgical family lounge. Through the glass, Amy spied Uncle Flynn and her father standing near a coffee machine. She whipped the door open and rushed toward them not knowing who to embrace first. Her dad took a step away from her uncle making the decision for her. She flung her arms around Flynn.

"*Mo doar*," Flynn said lapsing into his native Gaelic, *my dear* as he gave her a squeeze.

He held her at arm's length. His green eyes were dull and framed by worry lines. There was a grayish pall to his skin. The thin smile he gave her seemed the most he could manage. "If I didn't know about your play, I swear I wouldn't have recognized you."

"I'm sorry about this get-up," she said clasping Flynn's hands. "I didn't have time to change when I heard the news. How is she? What happened?"

His hands shook and his eyes glistened with a sheen of tears. "It's all my fault. If I didn't..." He bowed his head.

Danny draped an arm around Flynn's shoulder. "Nothing is your fault. Kay's going to come through this fine. She's a fighter."

Her uncle nodded his head. "From your lips to God's ears."

"Exactly." Danny gazed at Amy. "Mom updated about a half hour ago. They removed the bullet and stopped the bleeding. She's lost a lot of blood, but your mother is guardedly optimistic overall. She should be out of surgery soon."

"OK. Thanks, Dad."

He gently steered Flynn toward a sofa. "Maybe sit for a bit. I'll bring you a cup of coffee."

"I'll get the coffee, Dad."

"All right." Flynn stared fixedly at a color-coded digital screen above the reception desk.

Amy glanced up searching for Kay's name and status. Green, still in surgery. She dutifully fixed Flynn's coffee and brought him a steaming cup. She caught her father's eye and gave a head tilt at the door.

He picked up on her body language. "We're going to step out into the hall for a few minutes, OK, Flynn?"

"Sure."

"Text me if that color up there changes?" He pointed to the screen.

"Of course."

Danny shoved at the glass door and held it open with an outstretched arm.

She only had to duck slightly exiting the room under his arm. Her dad was almost a foot taller than her five foot six inches.

Amy huddled with Danny in a corner. "What on earth happened to Aunt Kay to make Uncle Flynn feel like he's somehow to blame?"

"She was out running errands and he asked her to make a stop for him. She walked unarmed into a robbery in progress."

Amy knit her brow and stared at her father who seemed uncharacteristically nervous relating the facts. In fact, he was downright twitchy.

"I don't understand. Why was she unarmed?"

"She wasn't on duty."

"Oh. Where did this happen?"

"Flynn called her and asked her to stop for a bottle of their favorite wine. A masked gunman shot at her as soon as she walked in the door of the liquor store. She managed to dive behind some shelves to get out of the line of fire and somehow called in the Officer Down. She was unconscious when they brought her in to Regional."

Amy blanched and teetered on her feet.

Danny preempted her reaction propping her up by the elbow. "You need to sit down."

"No, I…" She laid a hand over her brow. "Just give me a minute."

How could these circumstances repeat with someone she loved? Her father's murder was eerily like what had happened to Kay. *What must Mom be feeling right now? Please, dear Lord. Don't let us lose Aunt Kay like Dad.*

"Dad, is Mom Ok? This has to have…you know…"

Danny's eyes gleamed and his features softened: the lovely expression he always wore when the subject was his wife. "Her face was a bit pale when Kay was brought in, and she absorbed the facts. But the look of determination on her face? Let's just say that Molly Sullivan won't let the same thing happen to your aunt as sadly happened to your father."

Flynn rushed towards them. "She's in recovery. The surgeon is ready to confer with me. I'll let you know what I learn."

He strode down the hall on a bead for one of the post-surgery conference rooms.

"Let's go back to the lounge." Danny had yet to let go of her elbow.

Amy patted his hand. "I'm all right, Dad. You don't have to hold me up."

He dropped his hand and she fell into step with him back to the waiting room. She sat down in a chair across from him. "Where is Mom now do you think?"

"My guess is she's in Recovery and won't leave Aunt Kay until she's positive that she's stable and resting. We'll just keep a vigil here for a while. I don't know when or if anyone besides Kay's immediate family will be allowed to see her."

"Has anybody heard from Peggy, Amanda, and MJ? What about Mike?" Just saying his name out loud sent a surge of panic through Amy. How would he react to seeing her? He hadn't been to the play. Was he avoiding her?

"I know the kids are all on the way. You'll have to ask Flynn for details."

"Right."

She tapped her heel repeatedly bobbling her knee up and down in a futile attempt to relieve some tension. Waiting patiently twiddling her thumbs was not her style. She wanted to spring into action, do something productive and try to make a terrible situation more bearable besides praying that the surgeon's skills would prove enough.

Amy couldn't just sit there any longer. Her stomach growled in a volcanic rumble causing her to giggle. "Sorry. I haven't eaten. How about you?"

"No. I came straight here from the theatre."

"Well, then I have an idea. I'll make myself useful and pick up some sandwiches in the cafeteria."

"Sounds good. Thanks. Anything for me providing it doesn't have mayo on it."

She beamed at him. "I haven't forgotten. I'll be right back."

Amy strolled the hall and asked the cops that she encountered if they wanted anything to eat from her cafeteria run, making note of orders in her cell phone notes. She pushed both down buttons on the face-to-face elevator banks in the vestibule and waited for a car to arrive.

A ding sounded and doors swished open on Amy's far right. She hustled to catch the car and pulled up sharply as the man who haunted her dreams emerged from the elevator.

Chapter 3

Adrenaline surged through Amy accelerating her pulse, and she froze for a moment on the spot. Willing herself to move gracefully, casually, unaffected by his nearness, she paced a few steps in Mike's direction. Her spindly, high heel caught in a floor grate pitching her forward. His large warm hand gripped her arm preventing her from falling on her face and balancing her enough so that she could yank her shoe free. Still, she wobbled and reached out to hold on to his flexed bicep with both hands. Lifting her eyes, she gazed directly at the handsome face that she had fantasized about most of her life.

Her cheeks flamed. No matter how well honed her acting skills in projecting cool nonchalance seeing him again, her uncontrollable blushing gave her away. She dropped her hands, her arms limp at her sides and stood facing him. "Thanks for the assist. I'm not usually this clumsy."

"Amy?" Mike Lynch frowned shaking his head. "I had no idea it was you until I heard your voice. You're a blonde now? What the hell are you wearing? You look like a hooker."

She narrowed her eyes to slits crossing her arms over her chest. "Nice. You might have managed a more pleasant hello after not seeing me for years."

Mike's close lipped, crooked smile dimpled his

cheek. "You're right. Sorry. Hello Amy. It's good to see you. Why are you dressed like a street walker?" His dove-gray eyes gleamed wicked. He grinned at her.

She burst out laughing. "It's good to see you too, Mike."

Amy fingered a lock of blonde hair. "Wig. Obviously, I'm still in costume. When I heard about Aunt Kay I rushed straight here from the theatre. I'm surprised my dad hasn't roped you into going to the play by now."

I've looked for you in the front row every performance.

"I forgot about the play. I've been tied up. We just wrapped a case that I've worked for three months."

She'd be damned if she'd let him see how disappointed she was. "No problem. Just so you know; I'm dazzling in it."

"Ha. I have no doubt." He leveled his gaze directly into her eyes. "I plan to come see you perform as soon as I have a free night."

A bubble of elation burst inside Amy at the prospect. "Good." She reached out and pressed the elevator down button.

"Where are you going?" he said.

"To the cafeteria for sandwiches. Are you hungry?"

"Nah. I'm good."

"Okay. Flynn just talked with the surgeon."

"Yeah, I know. He's texted me with updates."

"Where are the girls?" she said.

"Peggy was out front when I got here waiting for Amanda and Mary. Mary's cab pulled up a few minutes ago. I just had to get up here." He rubbed his hand over his jaw.

"You go ahead. I'll go find the girls and then get the sandwiches."

He paced down the hallway, halted and then spun around to face her. "It *is* good to see you, Ames." Mike turned his back on her and strode rapidly away.

Amy stood at the elevator bank gazing at his retreating figure. *It's beyond good to see you, Mike.* Her memories of him were off. Certainly, he was more handsome now than she remembered. Was he taller? He had towered over her as she hung onto his arm. The fitted navy blazer he wore accentuated the muscles in his torso. His powder blue dress shirt tucked neatly into gray slacks. There wasn't an ounce of flesh over his black belt. Amy suspected that she'd find at least a six-pack under those clothes. She'd sure like to investigate that suspicion.

Mike had never attempted to take their relationship beyond "group dates" and, for her, one unforgettable prom night. She had no experience with intimacy with him.

She couldn't believe how lucky she had felt when he had accepted her invitation to prom. He had come home from school at John Jay for a long weekend especially for her. Every dance in his arms was magical and blissfully romantic. Amy had believed he felt the same way about her. They were both over eighteen years old. She had thought they were beginning an adult relationship. *The* relationship for Amy.

At age ten, she had first encountered Mike in the front yard of his house playing a rowdy game of touch football with his dad and his extremely virile uncles before eating Thanksgiving dinner. Danny had invited her and Molly to that dinner, choosing to introduce them to his family in one fell swoop. Even as a kid, Mike was tall, cocky and black Irish handsome. He was used to growing up with younger sisters and he effortlessly included Amy in the family fold with his sisters, Mary Jean, Peggy, and Amanda. When Molly married Danny Sullivan, Kay's brother, Amy officially became Mike's cousin by marriage. Amy had always viewed the Lynch/Sullivan clan as family – except for Mike.

The elevator door whooshed open. She glanced sideways and caught Mike watching her. She acknowledged him with a slight lift of her hand and then stepped inside the car. As the door slid closed, she blew out a breath. Even after years of separation, her attraction to Mike hadn't waned a bit. Did he know that he had exerted this power over her from the first moment they met?

Amy rode down to the lobby but didn't encounter MJ and the twins. Heading to the cafeteria, she ran into Trudy.

"Hi honey. I just finished my dinner," Trudy said.

"Oh. I guess I missed my chance to treat you."

"That's sweet. Thank you for the thought. Marty and I have been to your play three times. You're an incredible actress. The girls are coming home next weekend and we have tickets for another show."

"Why didn't you come backstage?"

"We didn't want to bother you."

"You could never bother me. Promise that when you take the girls to the show, you'll bring them backstage for the VIP treatment. I'll introduce them to Ry."

Trudy clapped a hand to her chest. "Be still my heart."

She beamed at Amy.

"I better get going. I'm picking up sandwiches for everyone upstairs in the waiting room. They're probably starving."

"I'm sorry about your aunt. I heard she's in recovery."

"She is. Flynn is probably with her right now. I think Mom still is, too."

"I'm going to check in with your mom now. I'll probably see you upstairs after my shift ends." Trudy squeezed her hand and walked away.

Amy grabbed a tray from the top of the stack at the cafeteria line and piled it high with assorted sandwiches, choosing a couple without mayonnaise for her dad. While she waited for the cashier to ring up her order, she dug her cell phone out of her backpack.

Ryder had called and texted. She typed a quick text to him updating him on Kay's condition. She paid the tab and then retraced her steps up to the waiting room, toting a large plastic bag.

Mike and her dad stood with their heads together, talking quietly. When Mike's father died in a car accident caused by a drunk driver, his uncles were ever-ready father figures – anything to help their widowed sister, Kay, and her children. Mike had become and remained especially close to her father, Danny, and relied on him for advice. Amy could only guess at how valuable Danny's assurances were for Mike in that moment.

Amy handed the bag of food to one of the milling CPD officers and drifted over to a seating area to greet the Lynch twins.

Peggy and Amanda jumped up from their seats as Amy approached. The duo enveloped Amy in a hug.

"You look amazing, *Sandy*," Amanda said.

Amy stole a glance at Mike who cocked his head to the side, openly eavesdropping. He winked at her. "Thanks. Your brother thinks I look like a hooker."

Peggy dismissed the comment with a wave of her hand. "What does he know? I'll bet her never even saw *Grease.*"

Amy nodded her head. "You're right about that. He hasn't come to any of my performances yet."

"Don't worry," Peggy said. "Mom will make sure he gets there."

Tears welled in Amanda's eyes. "I pray Mom will be okay and she's ordering all of us around soon."

Peggy circled an arm around Amanda's shoulders. "Of course, she will. She's already commanding our visits to intensive care and is haunting Aunt Molly to discharge her. MJ is in with her now. We'll have our turn soon, sis. You'll see for yourself."

"Do you mind if we sit while you wait? These shoes are killing me," Amy said.

Seated across from the twins, Amy appraised the identical, lovely, fair-haired women in front of her: petite and pixyish, so like their mother. *All grown up and poised.* "I can't believe that you last visited California *four* years ago. Where has the time gone?"

"Right?" said Peggy. "You have to stop by our new office while you're in town."

"MJ told me that you had finished all your classes and that you're opening your own agency. That's terrific. How's it going?"

"A bit slow but the office is set up now," Amanda said. "Peggy did the lion share of work while I studied for the Bar. But I've passed and now I can focus all my attention on work and holding up my end of the bargain at *Shadows Investigations.*"

"Congratulations, girls. I know you're going to do great things."

"Thanks, Amy," Peggy said. "Flynn has been a huge help. I don't think we could have done it without him."

The twins rose from their seats as Flynn and MJ walked into the lounge.

"Were your ears burning? The twins were just talking about you," Amy said.

He chuckled. "Lass, if my ears burned every time someone talked about me; they would have gone up in flames years ago."

Flynn gazed at the twins. "Your mom is waiting for you two."

MJ squeezed her sisters' hands. "She's doing well: still a little out of it, but it's hard to believe she was just in surgery. You go ahead. I'll wait here with Amy."

MJ gave Amy a soft kiss on her cheek, and then sat down on the couch across from her.

Amy left her seat and plopped down next to MJ. "What a crazy homecoming. You must be exhausted. Are you okay?" Amy massaged gentle circles on MJ's back.

"Honestly, I haven't had a second to even think. My phone lit up as soon as the plane landed. What a nightmare."

Tears tracked MJ's cheeks. "I didn't want to wait for my suitcase. I told the gate agent what had happened and gave her my claim check and requested delivery to Mom's house. I sure as hell hope they've done that, or I'll have to wear Ma's clothes."

She dabbed underneath her eyes with a crumpled

tissue. "I don't know why I'm crying. I feel so much better now after seeing Mom."

"You're relieved that she's out of danger. Go ahead and cry. Let it out."

MJ blew her nose with a loud honk which turned tears into a fit of contagious giggles that had Amy giggling, too.

Amy held her stomach. It felt so good to laugh after being so scared.

"Are you hungry?" Amy scanned the room. "I picked up sandwiches from the cafeteria. One of the guys has the bag around here somewhere."

"No thanks. I don't think I can eat."

Amy relaxed in the chair. Slowly tension eased in her best friend's company.

MJ widened her eyes and straightened in her seat, her rapt attention on something behind Amy. "Holy shit," she muttered.

Amy turned around and followed MJ's line of sight. Outside the glass walls of the waiting room, Ryder Scott strolled down the hallway with an entourage of two fawning nurses: Theresa and Mabel, Molly's co-workers in the ER.

"Right this way, Dr. Waverly. I mean, Ryder," sang out Theresa as she ushered him into the lounge. The sixty-something woman giggled like a schoolgirl.

Mabel was just as giddy next to Ry as her colleague. Leave it to Ry to turn normally stoic, unrufflable pros into star struck teenagers.

Amy stood up as the trio approached.

"This fine young man was looking for you, Amy." Mabel smiled up at Ry. *Did she just bat her eyelashes at him?*

"Thank you so much, ladies for helping me track Amy down." Ryder beamed at the women continuing to dazzle them. "I'd still be wandering around the hospital without your help."

"It was our pleasure," Theresa said. And then she just stood there gazing fixedly at Ry as if hypnotized.

"Um…" Mabel plucked Theresa's sleeve. "We should get back to work."

"Right. So nice meeting you Ryder."

The nurses dragged their feet leaving the waiting room.

Amy could hardly contain her amusement. "Wow. I see you recruited two new members to the Ryder Scott fan club," she said, grinning at him.

"What can I say? I'm irresistible." He wrapped his arm around Amy's shoulder.

"If you do say so yourself," she teased. "Ry, I want you to meet MJ Lynch, my best friend."

Ryder shook MJ's hand. "It's a pleasure to finally meet you MJ. How's your mom?"

"She's doing much better. Thank you for asking."

"After receiving Amy's text, I had to get over here myself. I was afraid things weren't going well."

"What do you mean? I told you in the text that Aunt Kay had pulled through the surgery."

"I was worried about what you *didn't* tell me. I thought you needed my support."

"Why?" Amy said.

He pulled his cellphone out of the back pocket of his jeans, opened the message App and showed the phone to MJ. "Do you see anything other than words in this message, MJ?"

MJ read the text out loud. "My aunt is out of surgery

and on the mend."

"Exactly. I rest my case," Ry said.

"I'm lost." Amy shook her head.

"MJ, please look at the other texts." Ryder swept his thumb on the screen scrolling conversations. "Do you notice all the emojis?"

MJ nodded and a smile bloomed as she apparently got his drift.

"Have you ever gotten a text from Amy without a heart or happy face or whatever at the end?"

"Now that I think of it, Ryder, no I haven't."

"Exactly. Now you know why I had to rush down here. Obviously, this was a cry for help."

"Sometimes you can be such an ass, Ry." But Amy couldn't suppress a smile.

He kissed the top of her head. "I've got your back, darling."

"I know. Thank you." She circled her arm around his waist and gave him a squeeze.

Amy became hyperaware of the heat of Mike's gaze. The easy physicality between her and Ry was purely innocent. However, if Mike interpreted that differently…good.

"I don't want to interrupt," Danny said, "but I need to leave for Headquarters, and I wanted to say hello, Ryder."

"Good to see you again, sir." Ryder shook Danny's hand.

Flynn strode over to the group. "I'm going home to take a quick shower. I'll be back in under an hour." He ran his fingers through his wavy, salt and pepper hair. "MJ, will you please coordinate sitting with your mother with Mike and the twins until I get back?"

"Of course, I will," MJ said. "Nice to meet you, Ryder. I hope I see you again soon."

"Count on it." Ryder gave MJ a hug.

"I'll drive you home when you're ready to leave, Amy," Ryder offered.

"Mike will take you home," Danny interjected. "I have some reports at the house I need him to pick up, so I asked him to drop you off."

Danny bussed her cheek and walked away; the transportation decision apparently made for Amy.

"All right," Ry said. "I'll see you at the theatre tomorrow."

"I'll walk you to the elevator," Amy said.

Ryder crooked his elbow and Amy rested her hand lightly on his arm. Mike's eyes followed her every move.

When the car arrived, Ry stepped inside and then turned to face her. "Why didn't you tell me that your best friend was smoking hot?"

"What…." The doors slid shut in front of her. "Now, *that's* interesting."

Chapter 4

Mike had made a point to overhear every word of the exchange between Ryder Scott, his family, and *his* Amy. He bristled at how chummy the man seemed with Uncle Danny. Mike downright boiled at Ry's obvious intimacy with Amy.

What did she see in that pretty boy? Ry had her back, did he? *Darling?* Since when was she anybody's darling... but his. All right, maybe he didn't have the right to claim her after years apart. Was he wrong by refusing to hold her down with promises when she went to California? Should he have told her what she meant to him then – what she had always meant to him? No.

How could he have lived with himself if he had prevented her from following her dreams? And look how well she'd done.

He was right to let her go without hometown entanglements: a decision that was affirmed with each of her mounting successes. Mike had followed her career from day one as if he headed her fan club. But if he *had* convinced her to wait for him to finish college, and maybe even stay with him in Chicago after he graduated John Jay, she might never have met Ryder Scott in the first place.

Helplessly watching her saunter away within the possessive circle of Scott's arm, Mike vehemently would have liked to prevent that meeting.

29

Even though her ride home with him was set, Mike was relieved when he glimpsed her walking solo down the hall toward the family lounge. The sight of her was both welcome and unsettling. He much preferred raven haired Amy to that tousled blonde with cat's-eyes makeup and ruby red lips. She flat out shouldn't be walking around in public in that outfit. The pants and top seemed painted on to her perfect body. The short, black leather jacket that she wore didn't hide a thing. He had always thought Amy was hot. Right then she looked like sex personified.

"Hey," she said heading straight for him, the expression on her heart-shaped face open, downright innocent belying her trampy costume.

Wasn't she aware that her swaying hips, her shapely legs flexing in those high heels, and just plain breathing in those clothes were *highly* provocative to any red-blooded male? The hospital floor was crawling with CPD alpha types.

He shrugged out of his jacket. "Here." He held the blazer out at arm's length.

"I'm not cold."

"It's a good idea to cover up anyway." Mike swung the coat out over her head and draped it over her shoulders.

She narrowed her eyes and plucked the coat off by the collar and held it out to him, the material pinched between her fingers.

He gazed at her evenly.

She waved the coat back and forth a couple shakes. "Take it."

When he made no immediate move to do her bidding, she frowned shaking her head. "What is *wrong* with you?"

Amy carefully folded his jacket and draped it over her arm with exaggerated care. "There. I'll just hold it for you." She looked him straight in the eye shooting him defiant daggers.

Mike looked up at the ceiling in exasperation - more to break the magnetic hold of her crystalline blue eyes than to convey displeasure with her. The last thing she did was displease him. "You're something else, Ames."

"So you've always said." She winked at him. "Looks like you're stuck with me. At least for the drive home."

"Yeah. Looks that way."

"Stay as long as you like, Mike. I'll keep MJ company until you're ready to leave."

"Uh..." He didn't want her to leave his side. From the moment she had almost landed in his arms outside the elevator, happiness had winged through him at the prospect of a second chance. She was home. Maybe she could still be his.

"Sure," he said.

She scooted away from him on a bead for the seating group where Mary sat bent over her cellphone. He enjoyed the view of her from behind, glad that she had refused to cover up. Mike had always thought her the prettiest girl he had ever known. When had she bloomed into the sexiest?

Amy did an about-face and scurried back to him. "Sorry. Here's your coat back," she said gifting him with a demure smile.

He took the jacket hanging over her fingertips on an outstretched arm and couldn't help smiling back at her. "Thanks, brat."

Amy flashed him a coquettish, feline grin before she turned her back on him again.

Mike drifted over to a group of Kay's men. "Thanks for coming, guys."

"No thanks needed," Bob Finelli said. He bit his lower lip shaking his head. "I only wish we'd had her back today."

"The Captain would give her life for any one of us," John Morphy said.

"And we for her," Finelli added.

Mike nodded expecting no less from his mother's brotherhood. And from her sisterhood on the force. He gazed at fellow homicide detectives Carol Finelli and Sally Morphy, rare husband, and wife CPD's who numbered among Kay's pride and joy. From experience, Mike knew that a sea of "blue" would continue to flood these corridors standing vigil over his mother's recovery. He also knew that to the last "man" they were chomping at the bit to get in there to see Kay. Hospital rules were meant to broken by these guys when one of their comrades was involved.

All eyes trained on the door leading to the Surgical Intensive Care Unit when it swished open. Peggy and Amanda emerged into the waiting lounge drawing over Mike, MJ, and Amy.

"Can Mike and I go in now?" MJ said.

Peggy shook her head. "The nurse kicked us out. Ma needs to rest. She could hardly keep her eyes open while we were with her."

"But she looks pretty good considering," Amanda said. "She can't have any more visitors tonight. I *think* they'll let Flynn back in to see her when he comes back."

"I'm sure they will," said Amy. "He can be pretty

charming."

"Or crazy demanding if charm doesn't work," Peggy quipped.

Mike rubbed his palms over his thighs. "Okay, then. We might as well leave, Amy. Did they say how early we can see her in the morning?"

"I'll check and text you," Amanda offered. "You guys go ahead."

He turned towards Mary. "Do you want me to drive you home?" *Please say no.*

"No, thanks," she said. "Okay if we all share a cab and I crash at your condo tonight, girls? Flynn doesn't need me in the way."

"Sure," came the twins' reply in unison.

"All right." Mike shoved his hands into his pockets. "You ready, Ames?"

Amy doled out hugs to Mary, Peggy and Amanda making him wish that she had continued down the line and ended in his arms. He remembered the prom date that meant so much to her in that instant. Maybe because that was the first and last time that he had enfolded her in his arms, the dance floor a perfect excuse.

A couple years before prom she and Mary had begun their obsession with the *Twilight Saga,* squaring off on the opposite sides of the "team Edward" and "team Jacob" ring. The "swoony romantic" prom scene where Bella and Edward pledged lifelong, vampire eternal love, had influenced Amy dramatically.

He had had no doubt that the adoring expression on her face that whole evening was genuine and meant just for him, and possibly Mike and Amy eternal love. But they both had college careers ahead. He had to return to school in New York. She had been accepted at the

California Institute of the Arts. The prom date was pivotal and meant just as much to Mike as it had to Amy – or maybe even Bella and Edward. The thing was, he had never given Amy a clue.

"I'm ready if you are." Her sweet, lilting voice snapped him back to the present.

He realized with a start that he had never heard her sing. She had to be talented, or she wouldn't have landed a starring role in a musical – especially one where Olivia Newton John had set the bar. Mike had spent much of his life secretly comparing any woman that he had known to Amy. He suspected that his memory of Amy as the gold standard of comparison paled against who she was today.

Seated next to him in Mike's department-assigned, mud-colored sedan, Amy tilted back in her seat and crossed first one leg and then the other over her lap shoving off the stilettos and thudding the shoes onto the floor.

"Ahh…" she sighed. "Much better."

She rummaged in the backpack that she had positioned in between her feet on the floorboard and pulled out a hairbrush. With one hand on the edge of the visor, she said, "Is it all right if I take off this wig and do something with my hair?"

"Be my guest."

He would have liked to watch her every move, but he had to drive and could only steal glimpses of the transformation from bombshell-blonde to, in his opinion, nuclear bomb sable haired. Underneath the wig her head was a minefield of Bobby pins. One by one she slipped the pins out of her hair and plopped them into the backpack freeing a succession of long curling tendrils around her face. She used the brush in a few flowing strokes and then ran her fingers beneath her tresses somehow magically styling her curls into perfection framing the porcelain skin of her face. The cosmetics were still overdone. Amy had never needed to use them to look stunning. But then, even with the stage makeup, Mike fully recognized the woman who had lingered in his dreams since he was a teenager.

Feeling on more solid ground, he relaxed in her company. "Tell me about your life now, Amy. Do you like living in California?"

"I do. You can't beat the weather and I just bought a home there. Makes me feel more settled."

"I know. MJ moved in with you, right?"

"Well duh. Of course, you know about the house. Yes, she's with me and I'm so glad. I've been lonely."

Me, too. "Really? Kind of thought that *Ryland*, whatever his name is, was taking care of *that*."

He rolled his eyes at his slip of the tongue. Mike hadn't intended to reveal his jealousy.

"Listen to you." She swatted him on his arm. "It's Ryder, by the way. What's it to you anyway, Michael?"

He smiled despite his gaffe. "I don't trust those conceited types. Just protecting you, Ames. Like I protect MJ."

"Huh," she huffed. "Well don't worry. I don't need *any* protection from Ry."

This was not going the way he had hoped. "Uh…good."

A fork of lightning speared the darkness and a loud boom sounded as if the sky overhead had cracked in half. Amy jumped in her seat letting out a little squeal, tilted sideways and leaned her head and a shoulder against him.

"Still scared of thunder," he said remembering how he had always provided the sanity to her and his sisters when they were kids during Spring storms.

He kissed her crown lightly. "No sweat. We're grounded in the car by the tires."

She didn't budge.

"We're perfectly safe."

Still Amy didn't raise her head.

"Unless a tornado stirs up. Then we're toast."

Her response was a violent shudder.

Mike burst out laughing.

"Not funny," she muttered.

He didn't tease her further during the rest of the ride. When he pulled into Dan and Molly Sullivan's driveway, the storm's fireworks had abated and had petered out into a light rain. Mike shoved the gearshift into Park.

"You're home. And the coast is clear," he said.

Slowly she raised her head and her huge sapphire eyes locked on his. That's all it took for shockwaves of yearning to pierce his heart. Her full lips were parted, and she looked so vulnerable, so enticing, that he almost threaded his fingers through her glossy mane to draw her close and taste those lips.

Thank God the porch light blinked on, and the front door swept open bringing him back to his senses. "There's your Dad. You better get inside before it starts pouring again."

Mike sat immobile, his hands resting casually on his thighs – outwardly unaffected by Amy Sullivan when what he really wanted to do was open his arms and his heart to her.

Amy bowed her head searching for her shoes on the floor. She stuffed the heels into her bag instead of putting them on.

"Aren't you coming in? Don't you want to say hello to the kids?" she said, facing him.

"Nah. It's late and it's been a long day."

"Didn't Dad say that he has some paperwork for you or something?"

"He did. Tell him I'll drop by early tomorrow on the way to the hospital to pick it up."

"Sure…" Amy's gaze lingered on his face. "Well then…"

She opened the door, slipped out of the car, slammed the door shut and bolted for the front porch hopping puddles in her bare feet.

"Those damn tight clothes," he muttered, shoving the gear shift into reverse.

Chapter 5

Amy had peeked at the audience before the curtain rose each night, disappointed that Mike still hadn't come to watch her perform. Two weeks had flown by since seeing him. Couldn't he have taken a night off to come to the theatre by now?

Time was running out for him to prove to Amy that he recognized how important this rare hometown opportunity was for her – for them. She had less than a month left playing Sandy in the *Grease* tour. Amy would leave Chicago, and apparently Mike didn't care.

That day Amy tried not to think about his abandonment and relished the day off from the play. She turned on the shower jets. The steamy hard spray baptized her as if symbolically washing away her frustration about one-sided caring for Mike. She lingered in the shower up to the last minute that she had allotted to blow dry her hair and dress for lunch at noon with MJ at her Aunt Kay's house.

Mom had already left for the hospital by the time Amy bounded down the stairs. But she had made good on her promise before going to work to whip up a pot of Molly's Marvelous Mix judging from the savory aromas emanating from the kitchen.

With the pot secure on the floor on the passenger side of the car, Amy drove to her aunt's house.

MJ opened the front door as Amy raised her hand to

knock. "I finally convinced Mom to lie down to rest. Believe me, that was not an easy feat," she whispered.

"How is she doing?" Amy followed MJ toward the back of the house.

"Good. Feisty as usual. She's a terrible patient. Patient being the operative word." MJ chuckled.

Sunlight streamed through Kay's kitchen windows casting a buttery tint on the cream-colored walls. Amy lifted the heavy pot onto the stove, set the burner on simmer and then turned around taking in her surroundings. Memories flooded her thoughts of the beginnings of lifelong friendship, her consuming teenage crush and blossoming love within these walls.

"It's so good to be back in your Mom's kitchen. I loved being here mornings after sleepovers. We ate your mom's chocolate chip pancakes until we burst."

"Right? Then we were off to your house to eat your mom's Marvelous Mix for lunch. Which I'm guessing, based on the tantalizing scents coming from that pot, is lunch today."

"Yep. You guessed right."

Amy sat down on a side chair and pulled up to the kitchen table which resembled more a work desk than a dining area. Stacks of folders, a pile of books and MJ's laptop dominated the tabletop's surface.

"Mom's improving every day, but she's far from her normal self. Look at this mess I've made on her kitchen table, and she hasn't said a word," MJ said.

"Wow, that's not like her *at all*," Amy observed.

Kay had demanded a clutter-free home from her kids, as did Molly. The girls were never allowed to make a mess in either house. Amy's pristine housekeeping mimicked her mom's: MJ's housekeeping standards, not so much.

"Mom's even flirting with retiring." MJ wagged her head.

"That's shocking. But… you know. I think that might be a good idea."

"So does Flynn. I'm not so sure, though. Don't get me wrong. The last thing I want is for Mom to be injured again. But being a police officer means everything to her. It's who she is."

"Nah," Amy countered. "Aunt Kay's identity isn't her job. She's always been a good police officer *because* of who she is. I'm sure if she retires, she'll find something else to display her superpowers."

Amy and MJ burst out laughing. As little girls they both had believed that their mothers were superheroes. As adults, they still did.

"What is all this chaos anyway?" Amy gestured at the clutter on the table.

"I'm poring over head shots and resumes for my project. I haven't had the chance to tell you. Bethany Chambers quit the movie."

"You are kidding me."

"Oh, how I wish. She got a better offer and jumped at it."

"What could be better than a part in your movie?"

"A part in Trey's next movie, of course."

Amy furrowed her brow. "How could Trey do this to you?"

Trey Ross, a notorious, Academy award winning producer/director, had taken a special interest in coaching MJ when she had first arrived in Hollywood. MJ had worked her way up from his Second Assistant to a co-director and then a producer with his mentorship.

When one of her films won an award at Sundance, her reputation had soared. Trey had kept her under his wing, but MJ had finally broken away with her upcoming project.

"He lured Bethany away on purpose," Amy spat out brimming with outrage.

MJ pursed her lips slowly wagging her head. "Absolutely not. He'd never do that. Trey and I are a team."

"I've told you over and over, Trey has held you back for a long time. He loves his Svengali roll and wielding power over you. He's getting back at you because he's angry that his wife, Nicole vetoed his decision to pass on *Rose of the Adriatic*. Not only that. She even gave you the money to green light making the movie on your own. If you ask me, and I know you didn't...," Amy held up her palm before MJ could object, "I think he's afraid."

"Afraid of what? Of me? Why in the world would he fear me?"

"He's afraid you'll succeed without him. I can't decide if it's an ego thing and he wants to take the credit for all your successes or if he legitimately might miss working with you."

"He...," MJ sputtered, cut off by her mother's sudden appearance in the kitchen.

Kay shuffled to the stove. "I smelled something delicious in my bedroom and I'm starving."

Amy shoved back her chair and scurried over to Kay. "Is it okay to hug you?" She eyed Kay's arm in a sling.

Kay opened her free arm. Amy gave her an awkward half-hug, delighted that she squeezed her back with vitality.

"You look wonderful," Amy declared. "Sit down and I'll fix you lunch."

Amy opened the cabinet where Kay kept bowls and the utensils drawer from second nature, the kitchen as familiar as her own. She filled a ceramic bowl with the spicy meat stew and then she placed the meal, a napkin, and a spoon in front of Kay.

Kay dug into the Marvelous Mix and let out a sigh. "This is so delicious. No matter how many times I've tried to make this myself, even though I religiously follow Molly's recipe, I fall short. I just don't have your mother's magic touch in the kitchen."

She finished another bite and then put the spoon down. "What were you two arguing about?"

"Oh, it was nothing, Mom," MJ said.

"I was shot in the shoulder, Mary Jean, not in the head." Kay leveled a penetrating gaze at MJ, exhibiting the Sullivan's unanimous talent as skilled interrogators.

"Really, Mom. We weren't arguing at all."

Kay remained stone still and silent.

"All right. Geez. We were talking about Trey. No big deal."

"What did he do *now*?" Kay shot Amy a sideways glance.

"Wait until you hear," Amy said.

MJ folded her arms over chest and said nothing.

"I already knew something was going on before I walked in on you two," Kay said. "First off, your phone has rung practically round the clock for two days. Which means something was or is wrong at work. Which also means Trey is involved. Second, you have made a complete mess of my kitchen."

Amy smiled. If Aunt Kay complained about a mess

in her house, she was truly recovering from her injury.

"Bethany Chambers left a message last night that she's giving up the role of Anna. She's decided to move on to another project," MJ admitted.

"She's moving on to Trey's project," Kay said accurately intuiting who was behind MJ's problem.

"Exactly," Amy chimed in. "And I just know that Trey lured her away on purpose."

Amy sat down next to Kay eager to have a possible ally. "What do you think Aunt Kay? Maybe he's vindictive because Nicole went above his head and offered MJ the money to fund the project?"

"I do think he's trying to undermine the production. I'm not sure of his motives. But I'm positive that Mary shouldn't trust him."

"I agree completely." Amy nodded her head. "He's afraid that MJ will succeed without him."

"He can be afraid all he wants. She *will* succeed without the likes of him," Kay declared.

"Hello. I'm right here. I can hear you," MJ sang out. "Both of you have Trey all wrong. He was there for me when no one wanted to hire me when I first came to California despite no practical experience in the trade. He worked side by side with me – true teamwork. I can't just throw that all away. I'm grateful and will always feel indebted to him."

"He did help you when you were starting out," Kay conceded. "I'm grateful to him for that, too. I hope I'm wrong about him now." She patted MJ's hand. "I just want you to be careful that's all."

"I'm not worried about Trey. Right now, my number one priority is replacing Bethany."

"Weren't you supposed to leave for Croatia to do

location shoots this weekend?" Amy said.

"Luckily, I had already postponed the trip for three weeks before Bethany dropped her bomb."

"You didn't postpone because of me, did you?" Kay narrowed her eyes as if pained at the prospect.

"Of course, I did, Mom. How could I even think of leaving the country until I knew you were all right?"

"I'm so sorry," Kay said.

MJ waved the sentiment off. "No need to apologize *at all*. It worked out perfectly. Now I have time to find the perfect person to play Anna."

"Any good candidates?" Amy said.

"Not yet."

Kay wagged her head. "Sometimes, Mary Jean, you can't see the forest for the..."

A motor groaned from off the kitchen and a rumbling sounded as the garage door opened along the track.

Kay broke into a smile. "Flynn's home early." She rose to her feet steadying her balance with a hand on the table.

Amy preempted Kay's clearing the table by picking up the bowl. "I've got it, Aunt Kay. You go say hello to Flynn."

"Thank you, Honey." Kay bent to kiss the top of MJ's head as she passed her daughter. "Don't be mad at me. I just want the best for you."

"Oh, Mom I know that. I could never be mad at you."

MJ's phone vibrated on the table. She glanced at the screen, hit decline, and rubbed her hand over her face. "I'm too tired to manage this, but my mind races every time I get in bed; and I can't sleep at all."

"You can't go on like this. You'll have a breakdown," Amy said. "Remember how Grandma always said that the best way to tackle a problem is to make a list? Whenever I followed that advice, I always felt grounded to tackle any task. I use so many of her life lessons every day. Let's make a list of what you need done."

Amy rummaged through the folders on the table until she found a blank pad of paper. She sat down next to MJ and wrote the number one on the first page of the pad. "I know the first thing you want to do is find a new Anna. Let that sit for a while. What do you have to do next?"

"I need to change the hotel reservations for the crew. And check to make sure we can still take some of the planned location shots."

"I can help with the calls." Amy dug in her backpack and pulled out a dog-eared copy of the script for *Rose of the Adriatic*.

MJ stopped scrolling on her phone and stared at Amy. "You have a copy of the script?"

"You gave it to me, remember?"

MJ cast her eyes downward in concentration then slowly nodded her head. "I do remember. You told me you wanted to read it. You never said if you did or not."

"I brought it on the plane and couldn't put it down. I've read it about three times so far. I had to see how you'd turn the book into a movie. You know I loved the book so much."

"What do you think of the script?"

"I think it's perfect, maybe even a step up from the book. Honestly, I don't know why Bethany would bail. I get chills thinking about this movie. Remember when we were little, and we practiced our Oscar speeches?"

MJ grinned at her. "Yep."

"Well, my dearest friend. I think you better rewrite yours."

Chapter 6

Amy checked the time on her cell phone's digital readout and calculated seven hours ahead in the Adriatic region. She decided that six in the evening wasn't too late for a ringing telephone and placed the call to *Mir* House. Expecting to leave a voicemail message, she was thrown off script when Matt Robbins himself answered the call.

"Dr. Robbins here," he said.

"Oh…" Amy was tongue tied, caught up in a spell of hero worship. M.D., PhD., Matthew Robbins' famed work at *Mir* House and the miraculous circumstances that surrounded him there had captivated the world. The book, and now screenplay, *Rose of the Adriatic* was based on his love story with Anna, one of the in-the-news Marian visionaries in a tiny, sheltered village ringed by mountains overlooking the Adriatic Sea. His skepticism about her visions and his quest to disprove them had led him to a stunning truth about sweet, unassuming Anna. Her experiences and the myriad of miracles associated with them could not be discredited by any empirical means available to him or any other of his fellow scientists. God knew, he had tried.

"I'm sorry…I didn't expect you to answer the phone," Amy stammered. "I thought I'd leave a message."

"Well, here I am," he said pleasantly. "If it rings, I

answer. Who may I ask is calling?"

"My name is Amy Jordan Sullivan and—"

"Oh wow. My wife Anna and I are big fans, Miss Jordan Sullivan," he interjected. "Wait until I tell her that you called here. What can I do for you?"

Amy grinned, beyond flattered. "Thank you so much, Dr. Robbins. I'm highly complimented that you're familiar with my work. The fandom is mutual. I loved reading your story and have supported your work at *Mir* House with donations ever since."

"Now it's my turn to thank you."

"I'm calling regarding your story and the upcoming movie based on your experiences. I'm working with my cousin, MJ Lynch to arrange the revised location shoots. I take it you already were informed of the delay because her mother was injured?"

"Yes, we were. How is she faring? Anna has kept her in her prayers."

"That is so special. I'll be sure to tell her. She's recovering nicely. Since she's my aunt, I'm very close to the situation and I'm glad that my work has taken me to Chicago so that I can help with her care however I can."

"Why Chicago? By the way, that's my hometown, too. I love the Windy City."

"Of course, I remember that. I'm playing the character Sandy in a revival tour of *Grease* at The Chicago Theatre."

"Love that venue. I would like to bring Anna there someday."

"I hope I'm here to greet you if you do. Regarding the new schedule for MJ's project: I assume that you don't have a problem with the three-week delay?"

"Correct. No problem at all. You'll find we're

mostly a laid-back little village. If you don't count the hordes of pilgrims that descend upon us." He let out a hearty guffaw.

Amy instantly liked the man and wished she could meet him. How amazing it would be to spend time with a couple that bridged heaven and earth. *Hmm. Maybe MJ will let me tag along on the trip.*

"I'll let MJ know that she can proceed with her crew. I have a copy of the schedule I'd like to send you."

"Of course. Email or text is fine. Will I have the chance to meet you in a few weeks?"

The timing would work perfectly for her. She had planned to take a break after *Grease* anyway. Why not? She'd invite herself on the trip, if nothing else, to keep MJ company and meet the fascinating Robbins couple.

"It's not definite yet, but hopefully, yes," she said.

"Excellent. Anna will be thrilled. Hopefully I'll see you soon." He ended the call.

The idea of joining the trip grew on Amy as she dressed in jeans for lunch with MJ at one of their favorite childhood haunts – the mall. As teenagers they had relished days off from school so that they could hang out at the mall all day. There was a bowling alley, a miniature golf course, an arcade, food vendors and restaurants galore, and of course, shops and department stores to occupy their time.

They planned to simply eat at a restaurant. But maybe they would find time to fit in a little shopping before Amy needed to head downtown to the theatre for that night's performance.

Amy found the perfect parking space mere steps from the front of the restaurant. Her good fortune continued as MJ rounded the walkway leading to the entrance right when Amy reached the door. She linked arms with MJ and waltzed inside.

The minute they were seated in a booth, MJ fired off questions. "Were you able to connect with anyone on the Salvation Mountain shoot? How about Gospa Hill? The rose garden? *Mir* House? The church where Anna and Matt were married?"

"There isn't a problem with any of those sites. I spoke with Matt Robbins personally an hour ago. What a lovely man. You're all set, MJ."

"Really?" MJ sagged in her seat. "What a relief. Thank you so much, Amy. That takes a huge weight off my shoulders."

"Glad to help. It was wonderful talking with the real-life hero of your movie. How was your day so far? How's Aunt Kay doing?"

MJ's eyes shone with affection at the mention of her mother's name. She and Kay enjoyed a special mother-daughter relationship. Amy had always considered her best friend status with MJ equally shared with Aunt Kay.

"She's practically her old self and is defying doctor's orders right and left. I think Aunt Molly is tearing her hair out getting through to her."

Amy huffed a laugh. "Mom is used to patients ignoring her medical directives. Just ask her about the beginning of her relationship with Dad."

"I know the story well," MJ said. "I think contrariness might be in the Sullivans' blood."

Mike's handsome face flashed in Amy's mind – his jaw tight, his lips pursed in prudish judgment of her Sandy greaser-girl costume at the hospital. "You can say that again."

Amy leaned her forearms on the booth's wooden

table drawing closer to MJ. "So...I was thinking - how would you feel about my going on the trip to Valselo with you? My obligation to the tour will be over and I haven't committed to take a new role in California."

MJ's eyes lit with her smile. "You're a mind reader, I swear. I'd love for you to come – for a bunch of reasons."

"That's wonderful. I can't wait to meet Anna and Matt and all the characters in the book. Plus, if you have any free time, we can have fun together. Maybe a little tourism. Have you ever been to Dubrovnik? It's called the Jewel of the Adriatic. I've always wanted to go there. MJ, this is really exciting."

"It is. We'll have a great time. Amy, I had an idea. Mom said it was silly that I didn't suggest this the minute Bethany quit. Um..." MJ toyed with the straw in her water glass. "How would you feel about taking Bethany's place and playing the role of Anna? I'll work through your agent and make a proper offer if you're interested. I think you'd like the terms including a share of the box office..."

Amy raised her palm toward MJ. "Slow down, sweetie. Huh...This would be a plum role for me. I've never carried a movie before. Are you sure you don't want to screen test actresses – including me – before you decide?"

She gave Amy a crooked grin. "Does that mean you *are* interested? Even though this is my first solo project?"

"Are you kidding? I have every confidence in you. This will be a blockbuster."

MJ reached over the table and squeezed Amy's hand. "Ditto, sis. I have every confidence that if you play

Anna, you'll help me make a blockbuster. No screen test needed."

Amy turned MJ's handhold into a hearty handshake. "Deal. Oh my gosh, MJ. I can't believe that we'll get to work together."

"Want to have a glass of wine to toast our collaboration?"

"I perform tonight. I probably shouldn't…oh what the heck. One glass won't hurt."

Amy decided to forego shopping at the mall after lunch to leave for the theatre earlier and catch a nap in her dressing room before taking the stage that night. MJ had said that she'd make the arrangements for airline reservations and see about Amy's hotel room for the Valselo trip.

Backstage pre-show preparations were already underway. The lighting crew and stagehands bustled about working in unspoken unison. Her dressing room provided a peaceful oasis. Amy slipped out of her jeans and sweater and wrapped herself in a robe. She was asleep minutes after stretching out on the sofa bed.

The clockwork appearance of her dresser and makeup artist awakened her. Relaxing in front of the lighted mirror, Amy submitted to the ministrations that transformed her into character.

With Ground Hog's Day repetition Ry made a break-a-leg visit, flowers were delivered and positioned around the dressing room, Amy gazed in the mirror one last time making sure that no telltale strands of black hair escaped the cap beneath her blonde wig and then sauntered along with her ensemble separating backstage right and backstage left positions for the opening number.

Peering out a chink of open curtain, Amy met with familiar disappointment. A few CPD *Grease* diehards had already occupied several front row seats, but Mike still wasn't among them.

She sighed, resigned that her career might always stand in the way of having a future with Homicide Detective Michael Lynch. Much as she resisted, Amy got the message and vowed not to torture herself like that before her remaining performances.

The orchestra struck up the overture and yet again, Amy relished listening to the infectious musical score and geared up to make that music herself.

She hit her mark onstage in front of the bleachers where the Pink Ladies perched in rows. Ry stood on his mark in front of the boys' bleachers, loose-limbed and Danny Zuko cocksure. He gave her a wink and then faced the red velvet curtain. The curtain rose, the lights went up and she and Ry stood in pools of illumination amid the brilliant spotlights beamed from overhead. The orchestra played several lead-in bars of the melody while applause boomed in the theatre and then the music swelled for the opening number, *Summer Nights*.

Beyond the footlights' glare Amy spied sideways, shadowed movement out of the corner of her eye. Mike inched his way to a seat in the middle of the front row. Ry took up his solo part freeing Amy to flick a glance at Mike. Her eyes met Mike's as a slow, sexy smile bloomed on his face. Her heart somersaulted in her chest and adrenaline surged through her far beyond the normal dose that taking the stage brought. She had waited impatiently for him to care enough to come to the theatre where he might appreciate how hard she'd worked – how far she'd come since she'd left for California despite how he'd alienated her from his life. She poured all she had into her performance, determined to impress him.

Chapter 7

Mike was transfixed and utterly wowed by Amy's performance, and he regretted having waited so long to see her in action. That woman up there on the stage held no resemblance to his Amy, and he had to remind himself often during the show that he knew the actress playing Sandy. The transformation was so complete, and Amy's voice was so beautiful, that it appeared as if Olivia Newton John had resurrected and reprised her role in front of Mike's eyes.

He rose to his feet exuberantly clapping when the house lights raised at the finale. The cast took their bows in succession until Danny Zuko and Sandy skipped into view hand in hand bringing the house down. The ensemble launched into an encore, took a final bow in a chorus line, and then exited the stage.

His detective shield gained Mike access to backstage. Given directions by a stagehand, he headed to Amy's dressing room clutching a bouquet which thankfully hadn't wilted during the show. Her dressing room door stood ajar. He spied Amy's refection in a square mirror rimmed by light bulbs. A woman tugged off the blonde wig on Amy's head and she giggled at something the woman said. Vases of yellow roses were placed on seemingly every flat surface in the room.

"Margie, do you smell lilies of the valley?" Amy

said.

Mike glanced down at the bouquet in his hand and then ahead at the vanity's mirror locking eyes with Amy. He held up the bouquet giving her a smile.

"Oh wow." She rose from her seat and advanced toward him grinning. "Where did you ever find so many?"

"I have my ways."

She plucked the flowers right out of his hand and buried her nose in the star-like white blooms. "Oh, these smell so lovely. Thank you so much. They're my favorite."

"I know."

"I can't believe you remembered."

Her soft voice touched that part of him he had tried to ignore; believing, more like hoping, that his feelings for her would fade over time. They hadn't.

"I remember everything," Mike said.

Amy regarded him knowingly as if she could cut through his heart's shield simply by gazing at him with her sparkling blue eyes. For a split second he couldn't regroup to make his statement seem less like an admission of how much memories of Amy had always meant to him.

"For instance," he said seizing on a decent cover-up. "I remember the time you and Mary yanked out every single stalk of Grandma's lilies of the valley in her garden."

"Oh, I remember, too. Grandma forgave us right away, but our mothers went ballistic. We had to do all the chores for the whole summer."

She burst out laughing and Mike let out a breath that he hadn't realized he'd held. He wanted Amy to know how much she meant to him, but not by blurting his heart out standing awkwardly in her dressing room's doorway. *Soon. Before she leaves me again and it's too late.*

Amy tightened the belt on her robe. "I better get changed before they turn out the lights."

Mike wasn't sure if this was a dismissal. He took a chance. "Do you have plans, Ames? Would you like to grab a bite to eat?"

"I'd love to. I'm starving. It won't take long to change my clothes."

He eyed her vixen Sandy finale costume half wishing she wouldn't change at all. "Perfect. I'll wait in the hall."

Mike started to back out of the doorway but changed his mind. "Ames, you were incredible tonight."

Her eyes danced. "Thanks. I'm glad you came."

"I mean *really* incredible." He grasped her hand and squeezed. "I couldn't believe it was you."

She narrowed her eyes. "Huh. I don't know whether to be flattered or insulted."

Why the hell am I so tongue-tied with her? "Flattered…definitely, flattered. You're a great actress and singer."

"Well, then thanks again. Really. See you in a few."

He stepped away from the arc of the closing door and then leaned his back flat against it while his heart pounded in his chest. He couldn't let Amy go back to her life in California without telling her that he loved her. He had attempted, mostly in vain, to block her from his mind since she left Chicago. Occasionally, he had succeeded to dispel thoughts of her for weeks at a time. But then his uncle or aunt or mother had mentioned her name and her beautiful face had haunted him again. Tonight would be a turning point – either way.

The knob turned and Mike stepped clear as Amy opened the door. He faced her, struck speechless by her natural beauty without a trace of makeup on her face, her raven hair, porcelain skin, shining cobalt blue eyes, perfect body in tight, skinny jeans and… Mike couldn't stop gaping at her.

Amy fidgeted under his direct gaze. "Sorry. I look a mess. I…um." She twisted a lock of hair around her index finger. "I didn't want to keep you waiting. Should I go put some makeup on?"

"No, no," he stammered. "Sorry for staring. You look beautiful just the way you are."

"Very funny." She led him down the hallway to the stage door.

A throng of fans milled around outside calling out her name. He wrapped an arm around her waist and picked up his pace intending to protect her while running the gauntlet.

Amy slowed down. "It's okay, Mike. I've got this."

She slipped away from him, stepped within arms' reach of the agitated people, and proceeded to charm her fans. She signed Playbills, took selfies, and chatted up every single devotee until the last man or woman went away happy.

"Wow. Is it like that every night after the show?" he said once they were seated in the cab of his truck.

"Yep. But they probably wished I was Ryder instead."

"Don't sell yourself short. I saw Ryder leave while you were changing. They waited around for you. It must be crazy to have all that attention."

"It's unreal, but most times a lot of fun, too. Last

week Ryder and I went out the stage door in costume as preppie Danny and hot Sandy. The fans blocked the street singing and dancing with us. We had the best time." Amy yawned. "Sorry."

"Don't be. How about a change of plans? Would you like to come to my place, and we can order takeout and just chill for a while?"

"That sounds wonderful."

"How does Malnati's sound?"

"Perfect." She scanned the area through the windshield as he turned onto LaSalle Street. "I don't even know where you live."

"See that tall building just over the river on the right?"

Amy nodded.

"I live on the forty seventh floor."

He drove over the bridge, tires grinding against steel.

She arched her neck gaping upward at his building's facade. "You always said you wanted to live in a skyscraper downtown."

"You remembered."

"I remember everything."

Her echoing his earlier statement had him grinning. *A good sign, Ames. A great sign.*

Bolstered by that encouragement he opened the door to his unit revealing the vista that he most prized about living there. The city lights glittered through the arc of floor-to-ceiling windows; a sight that never failed to captivate him.

"Breathtaking," Amy said. She strolled straight ahead and lingered at the windows taking in the majestic sweep of high-rises and the shimmering Chicago River far below.

Mike switched on a floor lamp, strode into the galley kitchen, opened the refrigerator door, and checked the shelves.

"Would you like some wine? I have white and red." He grabbed the necks of each bottle and ambled over to Amy.

"Red sounds good." She read the labels. "Wait; I'll have the white. You can't open the red. That's a bottle of Jordan. It's too expensive. You should save it for a special occasion."

Mike put the white wine back into the refrigerator and opened the Jordan cabernet. "This *is* a special occasion."

He held her gaze, pleased at the smile that curled on her lips.

Handing her a full glass, he held his glass out for a toast. "Encore, Amy. You're a star."

"Aw..." she said tapping her glass against his. "That's sweet. Thanks."

She turned toward the windows. "You have an amazing view of the Sears Tower."

"It's the Willis Tower now."

"I know. But it will always be the Sears Tower to me."

She beamed at him, her eyes dancing triggering his heartbeat to accelerate. Pent up longing had him moving in for a kiss despite the risk of rejection.

Amy responded with unexpected intensity fusing her luscious mouth to his – everything he had ever imagined and more. Slowly he disengaged, afraid to push too hard too fast.

Her stomach growled as if yelling, feed me now.

Amy slapped a hand on her midriff, her cheeks reddening.

Mike huffed a laugh. "I guess that's my cue to order dinner."

"I'm so sorry."

"Don't be sorry. You're starving. I should have ordered right away. What would you like?"

"Anything works for me. Maybe a sausage pie, and cheese cubes. Oh… and their cannoli dip is to die for."

Smiling at her definition of "anything works", he made the call to place the order. "They said thirty minutes. I think I can scrounge up a box of crackers if you want something to hold you over."

"I'm good. This wine is hitting the spot."

He grabbed the bottle and topped off her glass. "Want me to show you around?"

"Sure."

Mike led her down the hallway leading to two bedrooms. High end fitness equipment took up one side of the smaller bedroom and he had his wood desk positioned in front of floor to ceiling bookshelves on the other side of the room.

Amy drifted toward the bookshelves that were jammed with books and framed photos.

She picked up a gold-framed photo of him, MJ, and Amy in front of the Sullivan lake cabin. Mike characteristically had posed making bunny ears behind each girl's head. "I remember this day."

He groaned. "I don't think I'll ever forget it."

She snorted. "MJ almost died of fright when you put that rubber snake down her shirt. I've never seen your mother madder at you."

"Add Flynn to the mix, too. That was thankfully the

last time that Flynn and I went head-to-head. I was grounded for a month, and punk that I was, I didn't speak to him for the entire time of the punishment. I learned a lesson that day. My mom is Flynn's Achilles' heel. You hurt my mom or make her unhappy and he'll attack."

"That's the way it should be. I want to be someone's Achilles' heel. I won't settle for less. Dad is the same way with my mom." She put the picture back on the shelf.

"Did you hear our uncles are considering selling the cabin?" Mike said.

"No, I didn't. That's awful."

"Yeah. I guess no one uses it much anymore."

"Remember the Christmases we spent there with the whole family together? It was chaos and so much fun. I really wanted that for my children someday."

"Me, too. That's why I'm trying to convince my sisters to buy it with me."

"Count me in, even if they don't want to buy it with you."

"Really?"

"Definitely."

"I'll put together a plan and let you know."

Mike showed her into his bedroom thinking about all those nights he had dreamed her right there with him.

"Wow," she said, "I expected military neatness like your old room, not so many books. And textbooks? Are you back in school?"

"I've been taking a few night classes working towards a teaching degree."

"That's wonderful. MJ never mentioned it."

"She doesn't know, and I'd appreciate it if we could just keep it to ourselves until I figure out if I can handle it all. I'm only in my second semester."

"I think you'll make an amazing teacher, but don't worry I won't say a word to anyone."

She spun on her heel, teetered, and stumbled forward.

Mike caught her before she fell, pressing her gently against his chest. "Whoa. What's wrong?"

Amy peered up at him, her eyes soft. "The wine must have gone to my head on an empty stomach."

Her gaze magnetized him as if time stopped. He tightened his arms around her, slowly dipped his head and kissed her wine-stained lips. Again, she ardently returned his kiss fueling his wildfire desire. He burrowed his hand under the hem of her hoodie and stroked the silken skin on her back. She wasn't wearing a bra which he took as an invitation to caress her bare breasts. She didn't object.

He leaned his forehead against hers, his arousal near painful proportions. "Now I'm the one who's dizzy."

She took the lead and kissed him, tongues tangling. Her hands inched along the waistband of his jeans fumbling on the rivet.

He drew her down onto his bed arching over her propped up on his elbows. His cellphone sounded in that moment like a blaring fire alarm. She jumped an inch off the bed beneath him, her cheeks flaming, her eyes opened wide.

Mike gazed down at her. "Sounds like the dinner bell."

They burst out laughing.

"What crappy timing," she quipped.

"Hold tight," he said. "I'll put everything in the oven on warm and we can…" He shot her a grin. "…pick up where we left off."

Mike punched the elevator button and waited impatiently for the doors to open. Pizza box and bags of food in hand, he rode the elevator back up to his condo determined to finally act on his feelings for her. He made quick work of keeping the dinner warm and then jogged down the hall to his bedroom.

Amy was sprawled on his bed with one leg dangling over the side, fast asleep.

Careful not to wake her, he removed her shoes, wrapped his arms around her and slid her fully onto the bed. He grabbed a fleece blanket out of the linen closet, wafted it over her and tucked the soft material around her.

He leaned over her and brushed a kiss on her forehead. "Amy, my love, you're my Achilles' heel," he whispered.

Chapter 8

A clackety, reverberating rumble quaked Amy out of a dead sleep. Sirens overshadowed those lower register noises – the unmistakable sounds of the city that suburban Amy had never awakened to before then. She blinked in the sun-striped room and sucked on her tongue trying to coax some saliva production in her mouth. Her lips felt stuck to her gums.

"Ugh." She stared at the ceiling working up the energy to leave the comfortable bed that smelled like Mike's woodsy aftershave.

Her stomach was hollow, and a dull headache throbbed in her temples owing to too little food or too much Cabernet Sauvignon; probably both. The longing for a toothbrush and a gallon of water overwhelmed her deep desire to roll over and bury her head in his pillow.

She rolled toward the edge of the bed, threw off her blanket and swung her legs over the side. Standing up gingerly, she surveyed her clothes: jeans and a hoodie that looked every bit like she had slept in them. Amy searched the floor for her shoes but decided barefoot would do for now.

Out in the hallway, she heard the whining hum of plumbing and the splashing shower emanating from the bathroom. The scent of fresh coffee and the promise of gulping some water drew her to the kitchen. She tested a couple of upper cabinets until she found glasses and coffee mugs selecting one of each. At the sink she filled a glass with water, drained it and filled it to the brim again. Drinking from the glass which she held in her left hand, she slid the mug over the countertop near the coffee maker with her right hand, picked up the carafe and poured a cup of coffee.

"Double-fisted drinking. That's my girl," came his deep voice from behind her.

She turned around to greet him and then sucked in a breath, temporarily speechless. Mike stood in front of her wearing only a towel wrapped around his narrow waist. When he had held her in his arms last night she had thrilled at the hard planes of his body. But *this*... hunky didn't begin to describe his muscular physique.

Her heart leaped. This gorgeous man for whom she had yearned endlessly for so long seemingly wanted her, too.

"I woke up with the worst cottonmouth." She took a sip of water. "Thank you for tucking me in last night. I'm sorry I pooped out on you."

"No problem. You were obviously exhausted." He breezed past her toward the coffee machine wafting soapy shower scent in his wake.

Mike filled a mug and then leaned against the counter opposite Amy in the galley kitchen, sipping coffee and steadily gazing into her eyes.

Amy was sorely tempted to take a few steps closer to him so that she could run her hands over those sculpted muscles and see how securely that towel was tucked around his waist. The chiseled features of his face transformed with his roguish smile. And, oh that body.

Determined to match his nonchalance, she leaned against the counter, too.

"So…" she said. Her stomach howled with hunger, and she clapped both her hands over her midriff as if covering its mouth.

He laughed and pushed away from the counter. "Amazing what big sounds come out of that little body. I never did feed you. I know a place you'd like. Give me a few minutes to put on clothes."

"Uh…"

Mike had already turned his back to her and had swept down the hallway.

"I was thinking more along the lines of taking *off* clothes," she muttered.

She set down the glass of water on the countertop and drifted over to the windows drinking from the mug. The morning panoramic view mesmerized her. The Chicago River wound from a basin to her right in a steel-colored ribbon in front of and beyond Mike's high-rise. Tour boats and sail boats skimmed the water, idling while the Lasalle and Dearborn Streets bridges opened to accommodate tall masts. An El train rumbled along the tracks into the Loop. Traffic zoomed on the roads fronting and intersecting the River into and out of the business district. From her aerie, pedestrians like animated miniature figurines bustled along the avenues. The urban energy was palpable. Her headache throbbed harder.

"Do you have any aspirin?" she called out.

"Yeah. Cabinet to the right of the sink."

Amy gulped a mouthful of water and swallowed two capsules. Deciding she needed some freshening up, she wandered into the bathroom and closed the door. She found toothpaste in the vanity drawer, spread a dollop on her index finger and made do brushing her teeth. She splashed water on her face and brushed her hair vigorously. Feeling somewhat revived, Amy stepped out into the hallway and bumped into Mike.

"Sorry…"

He kissed anything further she had to say out of her mouth. Melting in his embrace, Amy forgot her headache and her empty stomach. She pressed against him and gently, sweetly let him kiss her senseless.

When he drew away, his soft gaze felt like a caress. "Good morning, Ames."

"Yes. It is."

"I'd really like to continue where we left off last night."

"Me, too." She arched her neck and closed her eyes.

He only pecked a kiss on her lips. "But I'm on duty in a couple of hours. I don't have the heart to starve you out of another meal."

She grinned up at him. "You have a point. Rain check, then?"

"Deal. Let's go eat. You game?"

"Uh huh. I really am famished." *For you.*

Amy gazed down at her feet. "Shoes?"

"I left them bedside. They must have gotten pushed underneath. Hang on." He spun around, sauntered away, and emerged from the bedroom carrying her shoes.

She held onto Mike's shoulder for balance, slipped on each of her shoes, linked hands with him and left his condo.

The aspirin had kicked in. Amy could enjoy the soft breeze off the Lake, the shirtsleeves temperature and the warm sunshine strolling the crowded streets with Mike. The only way to fully appreciate downtown Chicago was on foot.

She strolled along with him in a dreamlike haze. *Was this real?* How many times had she yearned for him to regard her as a desirable woman instead of an honorary kid sister?

Amy refused to think beyond the moment. She had always believed that if Mike felt the same way about her, together they could deal with her living in California. Nothing was impossible for true love.

Mike ushered her under the awning of First Thing In The Morning Restaurant towards a hostess standing behind a check-in station. "A table for two, please," he said pointing to his left, "that one in the shade?"

The hostess grabbed two menus and led them to the indicated table. He held a chair out for Amy and slid her closer to the tabletop after she sat down. Mike sat opposite her and smiled up at the hostess accepting the menus she offered. "Thanks."

He handed one to Amy and then focused on reading his menu.

Amy scanned the area. "Cute place. Clever name, too."

"Yep, breakfast only. I like this place. It opened a couple months ago and has been packed ever since. We're lucky it's a weekday and after ten A.M."

"What's good?" she said.

"Everything. The apple pancakes are the signature dish. I recommend that. It'll make up for your missing dinner last night."

"Good thinking."

Amy gave her order to a coffee-carafe toting server, who apparently had a great memory since she didn't write anything on a pad nor push electronic buttons on an iPad.

Mike ordered a poached egg, multi-grain toast and turkey bacon.

"I'm going to pig out on pancakes and you're going all healthy on me," she quipped.

"I ate most of your dinner last night. Trust me, I've got you beat in the pig out department."

He patted his flat stomach which had Amy fantasizing again about whipping off his towel that morning.

She took a sip of her coffee. "Mm, this is excellent. Thanks for bringing me here."

"Wait until you taste those pancakes," he said. "So, I've been meaning to ask…"

His eyes narrowed slightly as he gazed directly in her eyes.

Gazing levelly back at him, she sensed that the detective was about to display his interrogation skills. "What?"

"Are you still involved with Ryder Scott?"

Amy sat back in her chair. "Huh." She wagged her head. "We were never really involved in the first place. The answer is no."

"Not what I read."

"Take it from me, the celebrity press is way more fiction than fact. Ry and I have never been more than close friends. Anyway, he's not my type."

"No? Not into rich matinee idols?" A corner of his mouth upturned in a crooked grin.

Amused, she got into the game. "I'm more into working man law enforcement types these days. I must take after my mother."

His gray eyes gleamed wickedly. "Molly has excellent taste in men," he quipped.

"She does." She leaned towards him. "And so do I."

He didn't say a word. The tender expression in his gleaming eyes sufficed. Mike reached across the table and gently clasped her hand sending an intense wave of pleasure through Amy. The sweet connection was broken when their breakfast orders arrived.

She didn't want to break the charged, intimate connection with Mike, but the enticing cinnamon laced aroma from her plate was far too tempting. Amy couldn't eat her pancakes fast enough one-handed, so she withdrew her hand and dug in.

"Oh my, this is decadent," she said relishing every bite of the apple-tangy, syrup laden, buttery comfort food. "I don't think I've ever had a more delicious breakfast in my life."

"Stick with me, Ames. We Sullivans know Chicago food."

Amy paused eating, fork in hand. "You sure do. Remember when we were all introduced to Il Vicinato at Mom and Dad's rehearsal dinner? The Italian food there is the best I've ever eaten in the entire country."

"I believe it. That's always been one of my favorite date night places."

Her heart somersaulted, and a chill ran through her. Dealing with his preoccupation with her reported involvement with Ryder had her forgetting that things worked both ways. What involvements did she have to worry about? Maybe he was "dating" someone now.

Just look at him. He probably has had women hanging all over him. How many women had he wined and dined in the "that's amore" vibe of that quaint, neighborhood eatery?

She put her fork down, stared at her plate a few

71

moments, and wracked her brain to recall any mention MJ might have made of his relationships with women in the past and came up empty. Amy realized with a start that just because his sister wasn't in the know, didn't mean a thing. Mike would never kiss and tell.

Amy hesitated to probe. But she had to know. "Can I ask you something?"

"Sure. Anything."

"Have you been involved with anyone…or are you involved now?"

Mike furrowed his brow. "Depends on what you mean by involved."

"Um…" she faltered. What right did she have to question him? She hadn't lived like a nun these past years even though no man had ever provided true competition for Mike. Why would he have lived like a monk?

"I guess I don't know what I mean. Forget I asked."

His eyes lit with mischief. "Seven years is a long time, Ames."

"You're right. It is." She wrung her hands in her lap.

"And we're a long way from senior prom."

"Uh huh."

"It's not like I forgot about you or anything. But when opportunity knocks…you know what I mean?"

She closed her eyes and wagged her head, deeply regretting that she had embarked on this line of questioning. Amy waved a hand, stop. "I get it. Of course. So… how about those Chicago Cubs?"

He threw back his head and guffawed. Even though he clasped both her hands across the table sending a rush of hot attraction through her system, her heart felt frozen. She really didn't want to know about his past love life preferring to believe that like her, no one had ever stood a chance to win his heart.

"Ames, no one is you. Not even close."

Amy gazed directly into his eyes. His frank expression removed any suspicion that her devotion was one-sided. Her heart melted and her spirits soared.

"Thank you. I feel the same way about you," she said, wanting to climb across the table into his arms.

His eyes blazed with intensity assaulting her with the fierce desire to fuse her lips to his and unleash years of pent-up longing. Could they start fresh and somehow bridge the distance between them? Could they move forward living half a country apart?

She hung in his thrall thrilling at the possibility of a future with Mike.

"I never wanted to go to work less," he said.

"But duty calls."

"Exactly."

"Maybe we can see each other tomorrow?"

"I have an early shift and I promised Mom I'd fix her dinner. Want to come?"

"Definitely."

He signaled for the bill. "It'll be cutting it close, but I'll drive you home before I report to work."

"No need. I'll call an Uber."

"You sure?"

"Absolutely." Amy took her phone out of her purse and opened the App.

Chapter 9

Mike finally rolled out of bed after hitting the snooze button on the blaring alarm five times. He had fallen onto his mattress at 3 A.M. after a prolonged shift working a lead, and he'd rather sleep until he awoke naturally. But he still wanted to get in a workout and catch up on classwork before going to Mom's house to make her dinner. Because of the wee hours Op, at least he didn't have to report for his originally scheduled early shift.

Rubbing his hand over his face he padded to the kitchen and opened the refrigerator. He slipped out a deep, disposable aluminum pan, set it on the countertop, and turned over the two flank steaks marinating in homemade teriyaki sauce. He looked forward to grilling the steaks to make his mother's favorite meal. His father had made the same dinner for her every Mother's Day, so it was a sentimental favorite for her, too.

He returned the meat to the fridge, grabbed a bottle of water, and strode down the hall to his gym/office. He jogged on the treadmill for a half hour to work up a sweat and then worked a weights circuit. One more half hour on the bike and he could still study for a while before he had to leave.

Mike took a hand towel out of a basket that he kept on the floor, wiped his face, and draped the damp towel around his neck. Chugging a bottle of water, he checked his text messages before starting the timer on the bike.

"Darn." The reminder text from his classmate Connie made him realize he had to skip their study session that evening.

It was hard for her to find study time and he hated to cancel on her. She worked full time, had three children and her husband worked two jobs to help make ends meet. Free time was precious for Connie.

He texted back an apology explaining that he was making dinner for his mom. Setting the speed and incline he started the bike workout.

A few minutes into the ride his phone rang, and he touched his ear bud to answer. "I'm sorry, Connie. I feel awful cancelling tonight, but I promised my mom dinner. I'll make it up to you. Just name the night and I will be there."

No response came.

"Connie? Are you still there?"

"Um… sorry to disappoint you. This is Amy."

"Amy hi, I thought you were someone else."

"Obviously. I won't keep you. I was on my way to Whole Foods and wondered if you needed me to pick up anything for dinner tonight." She raced through those few sentences like a triple-speak auctioneer.

"I forgot to get the fixings for a salad. If you don't mind, could you pick that up?"

"Will do." Click. The call disconnected.

Mike shook his head. *That was strange*. He pumped up the music on his phone and lost himself in his workout.

Thankful when exercising was behind him, Mike plodded into the bathroom and turned on the shower jets as hot as he could stand it. Under the pulsing stream of water, the muscles in his legs and back began to relax and he surrendered to the reviving sensations for a while before toweling off and standing at the sink to shave.

Amy's frosty attitude on the phone nagged him until an ah-ha moment clicked. Was she pissed because he mistook her for Connie? *Yep.*

He smiled at his reflection in the mirror. "Well, I'll be damned; Amy is jealous."

****

Amy tossed her phone. It bounced on the bed and then onto the floor. She made no move to retrieve it.

How dare Mike accuse her of having romantic entanglements with Ry when all along he had a Connie?

She tugged a navy and white striped shirt over her head and tucked it into her jeans. Without looking in the mirror, she took the scrunchie off her wrist and twisted her hair into a messy knot on top of her head. She grabbed her backpack off the floor next to her desk and ran down the stairs. Good thing she had the house to herself because she slammed cabinet doors, one after the other, gathering what she would need to make Molly's famous popovers to go with whatever Mike had planned for dinner.

The sweet anticipation of seeing Mike again that was her first waking thought that morning had dissolved, and she toyed with cancelling the afternoon and evening at Kay's house. But… Maybe she could work on the movie with MJ as planned and then leave before Mike arrived.

Happy with that plan, she finished packing up the recipe's ingredients in case she changed her mind later and decided to stay. Amy hurried to the car before she changed her mind all together.

She breezed through the aisles at Whole Foods grabbing vegetables to make a large salad, milk, flour, and a large chunk of Gruyere cheese. The cashier openly stared at Amy during check-out.

With Amy's change in hand, the cashier said, "I hate to bother you, but are you the actress who is in *Grease* downtown?"

"No bother at all. Yes, I play Sandy."

"I just knew it! My mom and dad took my family last weekend. You were wonderful. We all thought so."

"Thank you. I'm so glad you had a fun time. It's a great play."

"It's my favorite. Would you mind signing an autograph for my parents?" She handed Amy a pen and a narrow brown bag like a sleeve for a wine bottle. "I would love to give it them to thank them for taking us to your show."

Amy bent to the task and signed her name with a flourish. "How thoughtful of you."

She handed the bag back.

"Thank you so much!"

"My pleasure."

She loaded the grocery bags in the trunk of her rental car and drove to MJ's house smiling. Recognition never got old and her whole mood had changed owing to the cashier's enthusiasm.

Flynn's powerful black RAM truck roared up behind Amy as she turned into the circular driveway in front of the former Lynch, now Dowd house. Kay, seated in the passenger seat, waved at her reflected in Amy's rearview mirror. Amy hopped out and met Kay and Flynn behind her car open-armed. She popped the trunk after doling out hugs to her aunt and uncle. Flynn grabbed the bags and carried them away toward the house while Kay remained standing in the driveway.

"You look so much better, Aunt Kay, but is everything OK? You seem upset."

"Oh, I'm fine, I guess. We just came from my doctor's appointment."

Amy's stomach sank. She was almost afraid to ask, "Bad news?"

"Actually, great news." But Kay didn't change her somber expression despite the positive check-up.

"Would it be rude of me to say, then notify your face?"

Kay huffed a laugh. "The doctor released me to go back to work."

"That *is* great news."

"It would be if Flynn agreed with the doctor. He convinced him to only sign off on my paperwork when I can pass a shooting test at the gun range since my right arm was injured. I'm just furious with my husband."

"I understand how you feel. But I know he's protecting you even though it may not seem that way. He was a wreck the night you were shot, and probably every day since. Just set up the test and nail it."

"That's exactly what I plan to do. I'm going to make that call right now." Kay turned on her heel and Amy followed her aunt's stomping footsteps into the house.

The kitchen was in disarray. MJ was on the phone and from the tone of her voice the call was not going well. She paced back and forth in front of the sliding glass doors. Amy emptied the bags that Flynn had left on the counter and tried not to eavesdrop. MJ tossed her cellphone on a pile of papers on the kitchen table.

"Problem?" Amy said.

"Oh, yeah. You're not going to believe this. Kerry just called. She was finalizing the schedule for next week and found out that all our plane reservations are canceled. No one knows how this happened. I have the Travel Department at the studio trying to rebook, but they're not having any luck. I'm starting to think this movie is doomed. Trey was right when he told me I was in over my head to take on this project alone."

"Stop that right now. Don't you dare doubt yourself. You've got this. We'll figure something out. Anna Babic's story is meant to be told. If anyone can fix this, it's your assistant Kerry. Let me check with Ryder. He might know someone he can talk to about international flights."

Amy pulled her cellphone out of her backpack.

MJ's phone chirped. She connected the call and then pointed her index finger at Amy - wait. Her frown upturned into a slow smile.

Shaking her head, she ended the call. "That was Kerry again. Nicole found out about the cancelled flights, and she's letting us use one of her father's company planes."

"How did Nicole find out about the cancellations?"

"Maybe Trey knew about it, or Kerry told her. Honestly, I don't know, and I don't care. I need a drink." She breezed over to the fridge and brought out a bottle of white wine.

"I bought this for dinner, but I'm not waiting. Join me?"

Amy nodded, yes.

She filled two wine goblets generously, handed one to Amy and clinked glasses. "Slàinte."

An hour later Mike appeared in the kitchen carrying

a large pan. The wine bottle was three quarters empty. Amy and MJ were seat-dancing on the leather couch in the family room off the kitchen while singing *Dancing Queen* as the movie Mama Mia played on the TV.

Mike rolled his eyes. "How many times have you guys watched that movie?" he bellowed.

"Only once today," MJ hollered back.

The wine buzz had doused *some* of Amy's earlier irritation with Mike – at least enough to stay for the meal. She popped up from the sofa, switched off the movie and joined him in the kitchen, MJ in tow.

He opened a drawer and grabbed BBQ utensils. "Thanks for ending the torture," Mike said. "You drove me crazy watching that movie over and over in Mary's room during sleepovers."

Amy hooted a laugh. "You used to wrap your pillow around your head."

He gave her a crooked grin – just enough to dimple his cheek, light his eyes and spark a tug of attraction in Amy's core. "Yeah. Didn't do squat."

"I'll make the salad if you want," MJ offered.

"That would be great, thanks." He piled meat on a whale-shaped platter.

"I thought I'd make Mom's popovers. Sound good?" Amy said.

"Yeah. Sounds great." His gaze sought her eyes and she refused to meet it directly, instead bending to the task of making the muffins.

There was someone named Connie in his life and, no matter how unreasonable, she felt betrayed. They hadn't talked about exclusivity, and after all the years of separation, why was she surprised that he was involved with a Connie? Hell, there could be a string of

"Connie's" for Mike. She shuddered at the thought.

"I'll start the grill." He opened the sliding glass door and stepped outside onto the deck.

MJ had taken over the kitchen table with her paperwork, so they ate in the dining room. Amy relished the perfectly cooked steak and the delicious popovers – her mother's recipe having never failed her.

Flynn regaled them with stories about his childhood in Ireland and they laughed at his antics recounted in his lyrical Irish brogue. Kay was still subdued, but she seemed to enjoy her husband's good cheer, their earlier dispute at least partially forgiven.

Mike sat next to Amy and his thigh brushed hers a few times during the meal. Her heart skipped a beat with each contact no matter how she tried to ignore his compelling nearness.

Kay produced huge bowls of berries and whipped cream, setting them down on the table. A chorus of groans sounded.

"I don't think I can eat another bite." MJ sat back in her chair.

"Me either," Amy said.

"I can," Mike said. "Pass it my way, Ma."

Kay obliged. "This is a light healthy ending to a perfect meal. Thank you so much, Mike. You made the steak *exactly* like Dad. And girls, thank you for the salad and the popovers. Everything was delicious."

She gazed at Flynn. "Now, if you don't mind, I think I'll turn in. It's been a day. You can just leave the dishes. I'll tackle cleanup in the morning."

"No, you won't," Mike said. "We'll take care of it. Get some rest, Ma."

Flynn stood with Kay and made a circuit of the table

hugging goodnight. He stretched his arm around Kay's waist and ushered her away.

"I need to check my phone first and then I'll help clean up this mess. Don't start without me." MJ went into the kitchen.

Mike took his phone out of his pocket and turned it on. Kay's rule of no phones at the table had persisted into adulthood for her family. Amy didn't bother switching on her phone. She rose from her seat and stacked some plates. Mike concentrated on the phone screen while alerts dinged repeatedly.

Amy tried not to sound hurt but her wounded heart wouldn't let her. "Sounds like your girlfriend is lighting up your texts," she said stiffly.

"Girlfriend? I don't have a girlfriend."

"Well then, who's Connie?" she spat out.

Of all the reactions, Amy didn't expect him to throw back his head and laugh.

She sped away on a bead for the kitchen toting a pile of dishes, mortified at her lack of restraint and humiliated that he thought the situation was funny. The last thing she would do was laugh in his face. Mike caught up with her, took hold of her arm and stopped her in her tracks before she left the dining room. He gently relieved her of the stacked dinner plates, set them down on the table and faced her, his large warm hands on the back of her arms.

"I'm sorry I laughed."

She wiggled to escape, but he held her tightly. "Connie is not my girlfriend. She's a fifty-year-old woman with three kids and a husband whom she's crazy about. We study together. I had just texted her cancelling. I was supposed to study with her tonight but had to change our plans so I could be here for dinner.

That's the only reason I mistook your call for hers."

Amy ducked her head averting his gaze. She felt beyond foolish that she had jumped to conclusions. *Face it, you don't think straight around him. You never did.*

Mike tilted her chin up gently with his index finger. His steady gaze bored into her soul as he brought his face close, closer, and softly kissed her lips stealing her breath away.

The kiss lasted a few moments, but suspended in that sweet thrall, time seemed to freeze for Amy. When he drew away, she wished time had frozen.

"You have no reason to be jealous. I'm a one-woman man, Amy. You're the only woman I want to be with."

"I wasn't jealous…"

He smirked. "Really?"

"Okay…maybe a little. You really mean what you said…that I'm the one…?"

"Really." He dipped his finger into the bowl of whipped cream, dabbed some on her lips and then slowly swept his tongue along the contours of her mouth licking it off.

Amy's head spun and her legs went weak. She wrapped her arms around his neck and pressed her body closer to his, wanting so much more than delicious steamy kisses.

He locked her in his arms while he continued to passionately devour her lips.

They broke apart rapidly alerted by MJ's advancing footsteps. Mike picked up the platter of leftover steak and Amy grabbed the stack of plates, substituting busywork for the raging attraction between them.

In the kitchen MJ loaded the dishwasher. Mike gave

Amy a head nod toward the dining room, and he pulled her into his arms when they were out of his sister's line of sight.

"Unfortunately, those message alerts you heard were from my partner. I need to report to the station. Walk with me to my car?"

Amy entwined her fingers with his and strolled outside to the driveway. After a lovely, pulse revving kiss, he said good night.

She stood in the driveway and watched him drive away until his taillights disappeared.

"You *do* have a girlfriend, Mike Lynch and her name is Amy," she whispered.

Chapter 10

"Brian Cole, Amy Jordan Sullivan," MJ said introducing her movie's two stars.

Amy gave the lead actor a spontaneous hug. One, he looked like the most huggable guy. And two, her character, Anna was a hugger. "Hi there, Dr. Matt."

Brian wasn't shy. He didn't hesitate to give Amy a healthy squeeze and then he grinned down at her. "Well, hello Anna."

His arresting round, navy blue eyes rimmed with long black lashes gleamed. His sandy colored, short cropped curly hair and muscular body made him a dead ringer for M.D., Ph.D. Matthew Robbins.

Amy's long raven hair mirrored her character's, the visionary Anna Babic. But she would wear brown contact lenses while shooting the film to color her blue eyes chocolate, like Anna's. She had practiced wearing them at home for hours at a time so that wouldn't pose a problem once shooting began.

"I'm a fan, Amy. I'm looking forward to working with you," Brian said.

"Same for me with you. I can't wait to begin filming." Amy turned toward MJ. "How do you want us to begin?"

"Let's start with a read of the prison scene where Anna and Matt officially meet. Do you need me to provide you with background for the earlier scene that landed Matt in prison?"

Brian and Amy shook their heads in unison. "No," he said. "I've read through the script several times."

Amy had read the novel, *Rose of the Adriatic*, more than once and had devoured the screenplay that MJ had written herself. "I think I have my lines memorized already."

"Great," MJ said. "You can sit, stand, however you're comfortable."

Brian pulled up a chair to serve as a prop for a prison cot and sat down, his elbows on his thighs, his head hung low – the dejected captive who had just been told by his mentor, Harry, that the one judge who was key to his freedom was absent indefinitely from the tiny village of Valselo. He paged to the scene in the script and spread it open on the floor in front of the chair.

Amy stood as if on the other side of prison bars observing him, her script in hand.

INT. PRISON CELL

Matt raises his head, a belligerent expression on his face.

ANNA

Good morning. Dr. Robbins, is it?

MATT

Who else? Throw many people in jail around here?

ANNA

No. In truth I can't remember the last time this cell was occupied.

Matt stands and moves closer to Anna meaning to intimidate her.

Anna holds her ground.

ANNA

Not very comfortable accommodations.

Matt's cold stare repels Anna, and she turns away.

ANNA

I'm sorry. I shouldn't have come.

Matt reaches a hand through the bars.

MATT

No wait. Don't go!

Anna turns around, pleased by the soft, remorseful expression on Matt's face.

MATT

I should not have tested you without your permission. I'm sorry I hurt you. Next time I will ask you first.

ANNA

There will *not* be a next time.

MATT

Why not? What are you afraid of? Are you afraid I'll prove that there is nothing special happening here? That none of this is real?

ANNA

I have submitted to the scientists and their tests enough. I do not have to prove anything to anyone, especially a rude stranger like you.

Matt steps back with a jerk at the affront.

MATT

You have everything to prove to anyone who comes here. You can't play with people's lives. Harry and Jenna would not be here if it weren't for you. My life would not be falling apart.

ANNA

I am sad for you if your life is falling apart like you say, but how could I be responsible? Would that not be your fault? Harry and Jenna are here because they were called to do their work. I did not call them. Our Lady did.

I live my life. I share Our Lady's messages with anyone who desires to listen. That is what I've been called to do.

MATT

You give them false hope with all your messages.

ANNA

They are not my messages. You don't understand. Gospa is warning the world with her messages of peace and prayer. I am just her instrument. You think you know me; you don't. I did not come here to argue with you or defend myself.

MATT

Why *did* you come?

ANNA

To tell you that I am not going to file a complaint. If I wanted to play with people's lives, like you say, I could keep you in this cell. Our judge was here last week. He will not be back for a while.

MATT

Harry told me that last night. He was going to try and spring me this morning.

ANNA

I doubt even my Doctor Harry could convince the police to release you. They are very protective of their own in Valselo.

MATT

Your doctor Harry?

ANNA

We're also possessive of our favorite newcomers to Valselo. He's a special man.

Matt nods his head wearily and sinks back down onto his cot.

MATT

I sure bungled everything. I never meant for any of

this to happen. You don't know me, either, but I usually think things through more…effectively.

ANNA

It's OK. I forgive you.

Matt opens his mouth as if to speak and Anna holds up a hand, stop.

ANNA

Do not put your foot in your mouth again.

Matt clamps his mouth shut spurring Anna's laughter. He gets up and moves to the bars extending his hand for shake.

MATT

Friends?

Anna accepts the handshake.

ANNA

Yes.

MATT

You have to let me run some tests…please.

ANNA

I will pray on it and let you know.

Anna drops Matt's hand and walks away.

MATT

Hey! What about getting me out of here?

ANNA

You can let yourself out. The bars don't have a lock on them.

"And cut!" MJ said. She clasped her hands together, her face lit with apparent delight. "That was the *most* on the money first-time script read I've ever heard. You guys are gonna be a dream to work with.

I can't wait to be on set. You're facial expressions, tone, body language? I wouldn't change a thing!" she sang out practically hopping up and down.

Brian and Amy grinned from ear to ear. "That was fun," Amy said.

"It was," he agreed. "I was pretty stoked when my agent told me I had the part."

"Not as stoked as I am right now," MJ said. "Amy. Let's do a run through of Anna's dialog with Mikhail in the last scene. I'll read Mikhail with you."

"Sure," Amy agreed.

Amy and Brian joined MJ at the kitchen table. MJ as Mikhail had the first word.

****

Mike propped up grocery bags against his thigh to balance standing on one foot while he levered open the handle of the door off his mother's garage. Inside the house, he walked briskly down the hallway towards the kitchen to put the groceries away. He had volunteered to do the shopping before his shift began that day. No matter how healed and back to normal Kay acted, Mike still wanted to pamper his mom for a while longer after her ordeal.

He heard MJ say, "You take my breath away," as he rounded the corner leading into the sunny, yellow kitchen.

MJ and Amy were seated across from each other at the table with booklets spread open in front of them. Mike quickly realized that a script was involved in MJ's and Amy's back and forth.

You take my breath away, too, Amy. And apparently, the guy who fixated adoringly on Amy's beautiful face shared the sentiment. *Now who the hell is this?*

The man didn't follow along in the script laying open at his place at the table. Instead, his eyes bored holes into Amy. Mike didn't like that a bit.

He purposely trod heavy-footed into the room and deposited the grocery bags on the counter with a thud.

All eyes raised toward the racket.

"Sorry to interrupt," Mike said, not sorry at all. He waved a hand nonchalantly – carry on. "I'll only be a few minutes putting away these groceries. And then I'll head to the station."

"We're almost done with this dialog," MJ said. "I want to introduce you to Brian before you leave. Can you wait a few more minutes?"

"Yeah, sure."

Amy smiled at him and then bent her head over the script.

First Ryder, now Brian. After the Connie-mishap Mike should have resisted assuming the worst about Amy and any other man. But…Connie never looked at him like this guy, Brian was looking at Amy. She *was* a beautiful girl who had become a stunning woman. Of course, men would gape at her with infatuation. Didn't change the fact that Mike couldn't tamp down jealousy where Amy was concerned now that he finally had her back in his life.

Besides, Mike still wasn't convinced that there was nothing between *Ry* and Amy. In his experience, he didn't believe men and women who had dated in the past could opt to remain only friends. Had never worked for him, *especially* with Amy.

"Flawless, Amy. Thanks," MJ said. "Anybody hungry? Let's take a quick lunch break."

She grinned at Mike. "Now that groceries have arrived."

MJ popped up from the table and placed a hand on Brian's shoulder. "Brian Cole, this is my big brother,

Mike Lynch. Mike, Brian is playing the male lead in the movie."

Great...are love scenes involved in this movie? Man, what have I let myself in for? One thing for sure, I could knock this guy into tomorrow blindfolded with one hand cuffed behind my back.

Brian rose to his feet and outstretched his hand toward Mike.

Mike paced the few steps to connect the handshake.

Brian pumped his arm. "You're the homicide detective, right?"

"Yeah." Mike shook free of Brian's hand. "And you're the actor. How long have you been making movies?"

Brian's eyes narrowed. "A while. I take it, you've never seen any of my work."

Mike shrugged his shoulders. "No, I don't recall that I have."

"Geez, Mike," MJ interjected. "What planet do you live on? Brian took home the Best Actor in a Lead Role Oscar for *Fill The Stadium* last year."

"Wow," Mike said underwhelmed. "Congrats."

He paced back to the refrigerator, opened the door, and began emptying the grocery bags stowing the food.

"Well..." MJ faltered. "I'm really honored that he auditioned for this role. He and Amy are powerhouse together."

The Oscar-winning actor wrapped an arm around Amy's shoulder spiking Mike's blood pressure.

"I couldn't agree more," Brian said.

The adoring gaze Brian shot at Amy had Mike clamping his teeth together.

Mike checked his watch, tamping down the impulse

to knock the guy's arm off Amy. "I better hustle. My shift starts in twenty minutes. MJ, could you please put away the cans and dry goods for Mom?"

"Sure," she said.

"Uh, good luck with my sister's movie," Mike said without glancing at the guy.

"Thanks," Brian said.

"I'll walk out with you," Amy chimed in. Her arms were folded across her chest, and she wore her you're-in-the-dog-house expression on her face.

Too bad, Ames. I have no intention of sharing you with another man.

"What should I fix you for lunch, Amy?" MJ said hanging over the refrigerator door.

"A sandwich, fruit, anything is fine."

"See you later, MJ," Mike said.

"Bye, Mike. Be careful."

"Always."

"Want to explain yourself?" Amy said when they were outside in Kay's driveway.

"Funny. I was going to ask you the very same thing."

She knit her brow shaking her head. "I have nothing to explain. Why were you so snarky with Brian?"

Mike ignored her question. "Do you fall in love with all your leading men?"

"What? Don't be silly. No."

"The press says you do."

"The press? Since when do you believe that stuff?"

"Hard to avoid when it's splashed all over the place?"

"Are you *kidding* me? The bigger the so-called splash the bigger the lie, in my experience. But wait? Are you saying you think I'm in *love* with Brian Cole?" She lay a hand over her heart. "Now you're just talking crazy."

"Yeah, well. You didn't see the way he was looking at you."

"Have you ever heard of *acting*, Mike. That's what we were doing in there, so you know."

"Pretty convincing if you ask me," he mumbled.

"Oh my gosh are we going to do this at every turn? I get bent out of shape over Connie, you over Brian. Don't you trust me at all?"

He heaved a sigh. Mike trusted Amy with his life. He always had. And he knew without doubt that she trusted him. But the woman had him all turned around and he had to get it straight.

The best course of action was obvious to him. He wrapped her in his arms and fused his lips to hers pouring his passion for her into the sweet, sweet connection. She went pliant in his embrace equally fervent, stoking the heat between them. If this was what arguing with Amy would be about, he looked forward to every future skirmish.

Mike ended the lip-lock only because duty literally called.

Amy hung on his arm, gazing up at him doe eyed. "Does this mean you *do* trust me, or what?"

"I trust you."

"And are we done with baseless jealousy?"

"Can't guarantee forever…but yeah."

"Good."

"I've got to go, Amy. We'll see each other when we're free next?"

"Absolutely."

He pecked a kiss on her lips and grasped the handle of the car door.

She lay her hand on his back and he turned around to face her. "Yeah, Ames?"

"Just so you know, I'm a one-man woman. And you're the only man I want to be with."

Chapter 11

Amy eyed the heap of clothes that she had piled on her bed assessing how to whittle it down enough to fit into her suitcase. Grandma Jeanne had taught two generations of Sullivan women how to pack only one suitcase for any trip length. Amy still heard her voice.

Now girls, you start with a midcalf denim skirt. Add three or four sporty tops. Next, you need a nice pair of tailored black pants. Then add some dressy tops. Add a few extra pieces that you really love and that make you feel pretty. Gym shoes are a must and, most important, bring a pair of simple black flats; they will go with everything. Add lingerie, pajamas, toiletries, and you're done.

Her cell phone vibrated.

She smiled reading the caller ID. "How many tops are you bringing to go with your denim skirt, MJ?"

MJ chuckled. "We thought Grandma's packing rules were fussy, but she was on to something. I packed to the letter of her law for the last trip to Valselo; and I wore everything I brought. I'm doing the same thing today."

"Me, too." Amy smiled appreciating their shared family history.

"I wanted to touch base with you about tomorrow. I'll order a car to take us to the airport at one o'clock. Should I sleep there tonight after the party and schedule the pick-up at your house?"

"That's a great idea. Bring your suitcase over whenever you're ready. I better run so I can finish packing. I need to be at the theatre early. I can't believe this is the last performance."

"The time flew, but I'm excited about our trip and working with you on the film."

"Me, too. What a wonderful adventure."

"I'll see you tonight. Break a leg."

"Thanks, MJ. See you later."

Amy dragged the largest suitcase she owned out of her closet and finished packing. She lugged the bag downstairs, intending to head to the kitchen to offer to help her mom who would host the family party that night celebrating the end of her Chicago run.

A knock on the front door sounded as Amy reached the bottom of the stairs.

"I'll get it, Mom," she hollered.

Amy had expected to find the caterer standing on her front stoop when she opened the door. But instead, Mike was at her doorstep holding out a single yellow rose in a porcelain vase.

She beamed at him, delighted at his surprise visit and the delicate, perfect rose he had brought with him. "For me?"

He nodded. "Of course. I'm sure you'll receive tons of flowers tonight, but I wanted mine to be special – the first. Not that you need it, but good luck with your last performance of this engagement."

"Thank you so much, Mike. It's beautiful," she said taking the flower from him.

"Do you have a minute to come in?" Amy stepped aside hoping he'd say yes.

"I'm all yours. I took the day and night off for the play and party." He strode through the doorway.

Mike stopped inside the entryway and swept Amy into his arms. On full display to passersby with the door open wide, he kissed her deeply. Amy didn't care about nosy neighbors or anyone else while locked in that kiss. His strong arms supported her body, gone pliant and floaty. He gently withdrew his lips, gazing down at her, a wicked glint in his eyes.

"Um…" She straightened her posture gathering her wits. "Well…that was a nice way to start my day."

"Plenty more where that came from," he teased.

"Good to know."

Amy nudged him forward and closed the front door glancing at the grandfather's clock in the foyer. "I have an hour before I need to leave for downtown. I thought I'd offer to help Mom with organizing before I go."

"Lead the way," he said clasping her hand. "Maybe I can be useful, too."

For the next hour Mike carried folding chairs up from the basement placing them where Molly directed and carried plates and cutlery into the dining room so Amy could set the table.

Amy replaced the floral arrangement at the center of the table with the vase and single stem from Mike. "Perfect," she declared.

Mike pulled her into a hug and whispered, "Yes you are."

She thrilled at the intensity she read in his expressive eyes. Amy cupped his face with her hands and kissed him. She had dreamed of his kiss, but nothing had prepared her for the explosion of emotions every time their lips met. Reality blurred, her heart pounded against her ribs and all she wanted was to linger in that breathless connection.

"Lunch is ready, kids," Molly called from the kitchen jerking Amy back to her senses.

He kissed the tip of her nose. "To be continued."

"Promise?"

"I promise."

The softness in his eyes filled her with hope that the end of the play wouldn't mean the end of Mike and Amy. They trooped into the kitchen where Molly had laid out a spread of sandwich fixings and salad.

"I'm sorry, Mom I don't have time for lunch. I need to call an Uber and leave for the theatre."

"No problem honey. I'll make you sandwiches to bring with you." Molly bent to the task.

"You don't have to call a car, Ames. I can drive you downtown," Mike said as he rolled a slice of ham and took a bite.

"Great. Thanks, Mike." Amy would never turn down a chance to be with him, acutely aware that their time in her hometown was rapidly running out.

Mike carried a bag of sandwiches and Amy's backpack out to his truck and Amy climbed into the passenger seat. Traffic was light on the Eisenhower, and they zipped downtown in a little over a half hour.

He pulled up directly in front of the theatre.

Amy twisted in her seat checking out the row of no parking signs. "I don't think you can park here."

He huffed a laugh. "I can guarantee I won't get a ticket."

"Well, duh. What was I thinking? Thanks for the ride."

"I had an ulterior motive."

"Really? What?"

"This." Mike planted a kiss on her lips, lingering just long enough to ignite a rush of desire through her.

In a sensual haze, Amy opened the door and stepped down to the curb. She gave him a wave as he pulled away tooting once on his horn.

As Mike had predicted, Amy's dressing room looked like a floral shop. Margie was seated on the couch ready to ply her trade with Amy's costuming.

"I can't believe this is the last show," Amy said. She dropped her backpack on the floor near the sofa and plopped down next to Margie. "I'm going to miss you so much."

"I'll miss you, too. But I'm positive you'll be back; and we'll work together again. You've been a big hit in Chicago."

"Aw, thanks, Margie. I hope you're right." Amy linked hands with her and stepped to her place at the dressing table.

Before long most of the cast had congregated in Amy's dressing room. Ryder arrived bearing a carton of champagne bottles and glasses. He popped corks, filled every glass and then he proposed a toast. "To the best cast I have ever had the pleasure of working with. This isn't goodbye. This is until we meet again."

"Until we meet again," the actors echoed, and everyone raised their glass.

Amy had tears in her eyes as her castmates left one by one to get ready for the show. Ryder collected the empties.

"My mom is hosting a dinner party tonight for family and close friends. Would you like to come?" Amy said, handing him her glass.

"Is your hot cousin going to be there?"

"As a matter a fact she will be. And just so you know, she'll be front-row-center in the audience tonight, too."

He winked at her. "Thanks for the info and the invite. I'll be there."

Ryder clasped both her hands and gazed into her eyes smiling. "Amy, I have sincerely had a wonderful time doing this play with you. When I was offered the part, I wasn't sure I should take it, but I am so glad I did. You're the best." He kissed her cheek.

Her heart swelled as she watched him leave her dressing room. Amy strolled unhurriedly to the wings wanting to stretch the final moments of tonight's performance. She could hear the overlapping conversations of the audience beyond the curtain as they filed into the theatre, and she relished the camaraderie of her fellow actors as they assembled for the opening act.

The curtain rose to a standing ovation led by three rows of assorted Sullivans, CPD officers and friends. The orchestra had to play the intro four times before the applause subsided.

After final bows and four curtain calls, the orchestra continued to play while the cast and audience joined in a sing-along. Only then did Amy allow herself to find Mike in the crowd. His eyes were locked on her, and she smiled. One more bow and then the curtain came down for the final time. The cast hugged each other and promised to be in touch. Phone numbers and email addresses were exchanged.

Amy was relieved when she escaped to her dressing room and removed her skintight costume. She had her make up off and wore a fluffy white robe by the time MJ and Mike arrived.

"You were amazing." MJ hugged her. "I've seen the play four times, and this was honestly the best yet."

"It was great. But I could have done without all that hugging and kissing with Ryder at the end," Mike said.

"Did I hear my name?" Ryder stuck his head through the doorway. "Hello MJ, good to see you again. Uh…sorry to interrupt."

"Good… uh to see you, too," MJ faltered, and a telltale blush spread on her fair cheeks.

"Can I have your mom's address for the Uber driver, Amy?" Ry said without taking his eyes off MJ.

"You don't need an Uber. Mike has his car. We're going to the party as soon as Amy's ready, and you're welcome to come with us," MJ said.

"Thanks. Let me just grab my things and I'll be right back," Ryder said.

Mike glared at his sister.

"What?" she asked.

"You could have asked me if I wanted to give him a ride," he barked.

"Don't be an ass," MJ spit out.

Amy burst out laughing. "Some things never change. Let me get dressed and we can go."

Laughter and a din of conversations greeted Amy as she entered Molly's house with Mike, MJ, and Ryder. Like all Sullivan family get-togethers, the men sat around the kitchen table and the ladies clustered around the dining room table. After hugging a receiving line of aunts and uncles, Amy filled a plate from the buffet and then took a seat near her mother. Mike didn't leave Amy's side, and Ryder was equally glued to MJ.

"Were your ears burning?" Bobbie said. "We were

just raving about your Hallmark Christmas movie."

Bobbie, who had lived with her after her father died and had taken care of her while Molly worked, had become like an older sister to Amy. Even though she had married her Uncle Joe, Amy could never refer to her as Aunt Bobbie.

"Thanks, Bobbie. I loved making that movie."

"Are you going to do another Christmas movie this year?"

"Yes, I'm planning to travel to Canada for the Hallmark shoot after Rose of the Adriatic wraps. I hope the scheduling works out perfectly."

"Great news. We had the best viewing party last year. Didn't we Mikey?" Bobbie grinned at Mike.

"It's my turn to host the next one," Aunt Matty, Brian Sullivan's wife, chimed in.

"Really? You had a viewing party? I'd love to come home and watch with all of you," Amy said. "Excuse me; I'm going to take my empty plate to the kitchen."

She rose from her seat and left the dining room. Mike trailed her.

Amy rinsed her dish, loaded it in the dishwasher, and turned to face Mike. "Viewing party, huh? I thought you said you didn't see any of my movies."

"I don't remember saying that; and the party was at my mom's house. There was no way I could get out of it."

"Did you want to get out of it?"

"No, I didn't." He clasped her hands in his warm, huge hands. Even his smallest touch sent electric shock waves through Amy.

"I wanted to see you, even if it was only on the screen," he admitted. "I think I'll always want to see you,

Ames. I want more time with you before you leave. Come stay with me tonight."

Amy trembled with longing. How many times had she dreamed of spending the night with him and finally telling him how much she loved him – had always loved him. Could she now? Should she risk her heart knowing that another separation loomed between them?

"Yes," she said.

There was no other answer. If she had refused, she would regret it the rest of her life.

Chapter 12

Mike swung open his front door so that Amy could pass in front of him into his condo. She seemed nervous and shaky. Did she regret her decision to spend the night together? Did she think by accepting his invitation she had agreed to be intimate?

He had no intention of pressuring her – ever. Mike would take it as slow as she wanted, for as long as she wanted. What he wouldn't do was ever let her go again. He hoped that she'd grant him more time to work out the logistics of living two thousand miles apart while building a future together.

"Why don't we sit for a while so we can talk?" he said, pointing toward the sectional.

"Yes…okay." She skirted the arm of the sofa and perched on the couch directly facing the windows, her feet tucked under her, facing away from him.

"I like the nighttime view with the lights off. Mind if I don't turn them on?"

She wagged her head. "Not at all. It's pretty this way."

The city's illumination haloed her sable hair and the skyscraper view through his panoramic windows made her look vulnerable and tiny as if suspended in the cityscape.

"Something to eat or drink?" he offered.

"No, thanks. I'm still full from the party."

Mike took a seat next to her and extended his arm along the back of the couch. He had obsessed about what he would say to her on the eve of her leaving Chicago, but he drew a blank. *How can we stay together living half a country apart?* Doubts plagued him, but somehow, they'd have to find a way – if she wanted him as badly as he wanted her.

"Amy…"

"Mike…"

Their openers tripped over each other. He smiled into her sparkling eyes. "You first."

"I feel bad lying to MJ," she said furrowing her brow. "She's staying at my house tonight and all I told her was that we were going for a ride and not to wait up for me."

"Hold on." He dragged his fingers through his hair. "Appearances to my sister have you stirred up?"

Mike withdrew his arm from behind her and slouched in his seat. "I give up."

"What?" She leaned toward him inadvertently showcasing her cleavage.

A knot fisted in his stomach at the memory of her tantalizing softness, the completeness he had felt when she had surrendered to his touch. "Ames, I'm stirred up, too. But trust me, MJ has nothing to do with it."

"Okay. Talk to me, Mike."

Amy brushed his cheek with her hand, and he clasped it, brought it to his lips for a soft kiss and then raised his eyes to gaze directly into hers. "I don't want you to leave me."

She winced. "Oh, Mike. I have—"

"You don't need to say it." He clasped her other hand relishing the electric connection simply touching her generated. "I know you have commitments with your job and I'm excited for you. And very proud of you. You're amazing. Really. I always knew that you were talented, but seeing you perform in *Grease*? You blew my mind. But this time, I won't let you go..."

Tears brimmed and tracked down her cheek. "Oh, Mike, don't. You're breaking my heart."

He brushed away her tears with his thumbs. "You didn't let me finish, Ames. This time I won't let you go without convincing you that your leaving is not our ending. I don't know how this will work, but I meant it when I said you're the only woman I want. That isn't going to change no matter how far away we are from each other physically."

Amy sniffled. Her eyes gleamed as a sweet smile bloomed on her lips. She flung her arms around him; and he embraced her, instantly ablaze with desire as she pressed her breasts against his chest.

She arched her neck and gazed up at him wide-eyed. "I want to stay together with you more than anything. Maybe you can break away and come to California from time to time? I will try to come home every chance I get."

"I probably don't have the right to ask this of you, but for me... I need to be the only man in your life, or I can't see this working." He kissed the crown of her head getting a sweet whiff of her floral shampoo hoping that the thought of exclusivity wouldn't put her off.

****

Pure joy surged through Amy. She had no difficulty wholeheartedly agreeing to his terms. Mike had *always* owned her heart no matter how she had tried to dislodge him by dating other men – she had loved only Michael Lynch from the first moment that she saw him.

"I feel the same way. Deal." She pecked his lips with a soft kiss sealing the promise.

He captured her in a forceful embrace turning her simple kiss into a whirling, dizzying fusion as his mouth devoured her lips. Their tongues tangled and she tasted yeasty beer overlaid with peppermint. He slipped off her ponytail elastic and threaded his fingers through her hair cupping her face while his kisses consumed her.

His hands slipped underneath her shirt caressing her breasts. Sensual spasms tugged at her core stoking an overwhelming need for more. She pressed a hand against the hard planes of his chest, and he withdrew his mouth, panting, questions in his eyes.

She answered him by whipping her shirt off over her head and unfastening her bra. Amy locked her gaze on his eyes which had gone storm-cloud, smoky with desire, stood up in front of him and continued the striptease shedding the rest of her clothes.

The appreciation gleaming in his eyes wildly flattered her and had her heart winging. She held out her hand in invitation and he bolted upright, swept her up into a fireman's carry, covered her mouth in a crushing kiss and set into motion. Heady sensations swirled through Amy during the brief trip down a hallway to a soft landing on his bed.

Amy watched, fascinated as Mike ripped off his clothes marveling at his chiseled muscles and toned brawn. He straddled her body on the bed and she thrilled as he slid his warm hands over every inch of her chest, caressing, teasing. He dipped his head and used his mouth and tongue to drive her into a frenzy. Nothing had prepared her for the onslaught of pure carnal need.

She was a virgin, and she should let him know in

that moment as they careened toward total intimacy. But she was incapable of speech as her mind emptied of every thought except more, more, more.

As if he heard her unspoken plea, he shifted to lave his tongue between her breasts, down her midriff, over her abdomen straight to her most sensitive center. Her hips undulated involuntarily, stars burst against her closed eyelids, and she moaned softly as a powerful orgasm peaked and then flooded through her with breath robbing intensity.

His large body covered her skin to skin as he fused his body with hers filling her completely. And then he pulled out in a rush. "Ames…" he whispered.

He propped over her on his elbows, locking his eyes on hers.

"Don't stop," she said moving her pelvis up and down against his body.

Mike stroked her cheek gently. "Are you sure?"

She guided him to fill her in answer. Amy would remember his tenderness the first time they made love – the first time she made love – as one of the most wondrous moments of her life. A tiny burst of pain was followed by wave upon wave of pleasure. How could such a strong, powerful man be so gentle? Her dreams of what making love with him might mean to her paled against reality.

He rolled off her fluidly bringing her with him to rest protectively against his side. All she wanted to do was linger there in that delicious cocoon forever. No work. No trips. No separation. No ambition. Just Amy and Mike making love to each other and then, maybe occasionally, eating or drinking something. Not remotely practical, but her idea of heaven on earth.

"Are you okay?" he asked softly, gently stroking her hair.

"So beyond okay. I'm wonderful."

"I didn't hurt you?"

"Not in the least. I'm sorry I didn't tell you before we went to bed."

"I was…surprised. You're so beautiful. I can't believe some man hasn't… that you haven't wanted…"

She laid her index finger on his lips. "I've never cared enough about another man to permit him intimacy. Not like I care about you."

He closed his eyes and a slow smile mushroomed on his face. In the dim light in his bedroom, Mike's chiseled features were softened. But she could clearly see that she had stirred his emotions with her admission.

Mike rolled onto his side and faced Amy. "I'm honored. I have never cared about any woman the way I care about you." He kissed her deeply.

Desire surged through her again. His arousal pressing against her abdomen confirmed the feeling was mutual. She stroked him intimately having never taken such a bold move with a man before.

In a split second he rolled her on top of him. He grinned, his teeth a flash of white in the shadowy room. "Have your way with me, ma'am," he teased.

Apparently, her instincts were spot on judging from his reaction to her every touch. "You're driving me crazy," he breathed.

"Good," she said relishing the newfound power she wielded over him.

Amy delighted in exploring his body and discovering how to please him. The second time they made love was equal giving and taking pleasure that ended in an intoxicating ascent together and a glorious freefall of completion.

Once again, lazing in his arms, Amy wished she could linger there forever. But the clock was ticking on their separation.

"This time when I leave, it will be different, right?" she posed.

"Completely."

"How exactly?"

"I have no idea. But it will be because we both want it to be."

"Do you think we could talk every day."

"Yep."

"Maybe FaceTime even?"

"I don't see why not."

She nodded. "Okay. We can do this, right?"

"Piece of cake. Get some sleep, sweetheart. You have a big day tomorrow."

"Okay…I'll just go brush my teeth first, all right?"

"Good idea."

They rolled off opposite sides of the bed.

"One more question, Mike?"

"Shoot."

"What am I going to tell MJ?"

He burst out laughing.

Chapter 13

Amy waved goodbye to Mike holding back tears. Again, she was torn between her career and Michael Lynch. She'd remain true to the whispered promises they'd made. Would he?

She used her key at the front door and slipped stealthily into her house hoping not to wake anyone – especially MJ. She tiptoed up the stairs. The light under the guestroom door stopped her in her tracks. She grasped the knob, took a deep breath, and opened the door to face the music with MJ. But the room was empty.

A slip of paper on the pillow caught Amy's eye. Sinking down onto the bed she read the note MJ had left for her.

I didn't want to wake you in the middle of the night, but I had to leave as soon as I learned that all my production equipment was loaded on the wrong plane and was on the way to Japan instead of Croatia! The car will still be there for you at one. I'll meet you at the airport, private terminal. Pack to go straight home to CA when we leave Croatia. I'll explain later. Pray that I fix this. LU

Another problem. Poor MJ. She had already dealt with so many challenges with the *Rose of the Adriatic* project, and they hadn't even started filming. Amy stretched out on the bed hugging a pillow against her chest. She fell asleep in seconds, dreaming she held Mike in her arms.

After a deep slumber Amy awoke refreshed. She enjoyed a leisurely breakfast with her mom before Molly left for a shift at the hospital.

Since she wouldn't return to Chicago from Europe as originally planned, she packed all her clothes into two large suitcases. What a luxury to bring anything she wanted on a plane! Amy waited at the front door for the limo which arrived at one o'clock on the dot. She wheeled her suitcases to the back of the car.

The driver scurried over. "I'll take those, Miss. Let me open the door for you."

Amy was poised to climb into the backseat when an unmarked police car, rotating beacon light flashing on the roof screeched to halt at the curb.

Mike bounded out of the car and jogged up the driveway. "I was afraid I'd miss you," he called out.

In the next instant, he swept her into an embrace and kissed her breathless.

She swayed on her feet as he drew away. "I don't understand. We said goodbye to each other before dawn."

"I know. But my mom called as I was getting ready for work. She mentioned that MJ will go directly back to California after Vaselo. I thought we'd have more time together soon. You didn't tell me."

"I didn't know until this morning. I was going to text you from the car." She smiled up at him. "This is much better than a text."

"I meant what I said, Ames. I'll do everything I can to make this long-distance thing work."

"Me too." Tears brimmed. "We can call and text

and… Oh, Mike." She rested her head on his shoulder her heart aching.

He pressed something into her palm. She looked down at the folded square of paper in her hand.

"I didn't have a chance to wrap this properly, but I want you to have it."

She undid the folded ends of the paper revealing a diamond cross necklace glittering in the sunlight.

"Oh, my goodness. This is so beautiful."

"It was my Nana Lynch's. I know she would want you to have it, especially going to Valselo."

"I'll treasure it. Can you please put in on for me?"

She placed the delicate jewelry in his hand and turned around lifting her hair off her neck. After he fastened the clasp, he planted a soft kiss on the back of her neck.

Amy spun and wrapped her arms around him. "I'm going to miss you so much. Thank you for this treasure. I'll never take it off."

"Text me when you get to Valselo." He kissed the tip of her nose.

"I will. Thank you."

She kissed his lips, yet another gut-wrenching goodbye, and rapidly climbed into the car before she dissolved in tears.

Sniffling, she fixated on Mike as the car pulled away. He stood in the driveway waving and wearing the sweetest, sexiest expression on his handsome face.

Tears streaming, she waved back with one hand wrapping her other hand tightly around the cross pendant.

****

MJ rushed into the luxurious cabin of the private

plane. Amy already enjoyed her roomy leather seat and a mimosa in a champagne flute on a table in front of her.

"What a shit-show this morning has been." She plucked Amy's glass off the table and drained it.

"Thanks, I needed that," MJ said plopping down into the chair across from Amy. "Thank goodness that Ryder has connections. We would have had to postpone this trip otherwise."

"What does Ryder have to do with anything?"

Amy smiled at the attendant who expertly replaced her empty with a full flute and served a mimosa to MJ.

"I was with Ryder when I got the call about the equipment and he jumped into action, made some calls, and had the equipment locked down in less than an hour. He's my hero."

"Your note said that you left in the middle of the night. You were with Ry then?"

MJ blushed a deep crimson. "We spent the night together. Don't judge."

"I never judge you." She laughed as MJ waggled her eyebrows. "Okay, maybe I do sometimes, but your taste in men usually is questionable. I'm happy about you and Ryder. You finally picked a good one."

Amy wasn't ready to confide in MJ that she had picked a good one, also. Maybe because Mike was her brother or maybe just to savor her rekindled relationship with Mike as her own secret.

Brian Cole ducked into the plane, took a seat across the aisle from Amy and MJ, and ended their personal conversation.

"Hey, ladies. Nice wings." His eyes twinkled as he scanned the cabin, obviously delighted with the turn of events in their mode of transportation.

The plane took off. After a delicious lunch, Amy and MJ slept for the rest of the ten-hour flight. A passenger van waited on the tarmac when they deplaned in the small airport near the Adriatic Sea for the half hour ride to Valselo.

The van turned onto a narrow street and then braked in front of a charming, white brick and stucco home. Amy was more than ready to get out of the car and stretch her legs.

Although they'd never met, Amy immediately recognized Katarina and Mikhail Lidovic, the pansion owners'and hosts of MJ's group. In *Rose of the Adriatic* the couple considered Anna Babic a member of their family and loved her like a daughter.

Amy waited for MJ to introduce her and then spontaneously hugged the Lidovics. "I feel like I know you both already. MJ has told me so much about you, plus I can't tell you the number of times I have read *Rose of the Adriatic*."

Mikhail's eyes danced. "That book has made us famous. Maybe good, maybe not so good. Ha!

"Follow my lovely bride. She will show you to your rooms. I will have your luggage to you shortly."

Amy and MJ unpacked in their sparsely furnished double room, bounded down the stairs to the gathering room on the lowest level of the house, and joined the rest of their group for a light dinner. Katarina and Mikhail were gracious hosts, and the food was delicious. After agreeing on the schedule for the next day, the exhausted travelers decided to turn in.

While MJ was in the washroom, Amy texted Mike to let him know that she had arrived safely and was in for the night. She was disappointed that he hadn't responded by the time MJ snuggled into the twin bed across from Amy's and turned off the light.

The crisp sheets smelled fresh and felt silken against Amy's skin. She plunged into deep sleep minutes after silencing her phone.

Amy suffered a bout of nerves about meeting Anna Babic as she, MJ and Brian made their way through a field of poppies. The visionary's home, a sprawling white stucco ranch with an inviting wrap-around porch, was located on the corner of the field. Anna and her husband Matt sat on the porch as the trio approached.

Anna jumped up when she saw them and hurried down the stairs, her arms outstretched. "MJ it is so good to see you again. Welcome to our home."

"Thank you for having us. Anna, I want you to meet Amy Sullivan. She's the actor we discussed on the phone. With your approval, she'll play you in the movie."

"You do not need my approval. It is my pleasure to meet you." She shook Amy's outstretched hand.

"The pleasure is all mine." Amy stepped aside so MJ could introduce Brian.

Matt had risen to greet them, and he shook hands with each of them. "Please come in. Anna has made her famous cheese biscuits."

They sat at a crocheted lace covered table set with delicate porcelain dishes laden with cheeses and jellies and Anna's fragrant biscuits. The food was scrumptious, and the conversation was fascinating. After an hour together Amy felt like she had known Anna and Matt her whole life as if they were family.

"Anna, might I please see your beautiful garden that I have heard so much about?" Amy said, knowing that a visit to the miracle rose garden was reserved for only a select few.

"I want you to see it. You all have more coffee; Amy and I are going to sit for a while," Anna said.

She led Amy through her sunny kitchen with lemon-colored walls, out the back door, down a stone path and through a gate into a walled garden. Amy gasped. A forest of rose bushes adorned with full white blooms surrounded her. She closed her eyes and inhaled the exotic scent of the perfect flowers. Never in her life had she experienced such beauty.

"Oh my..." Amy trailed off overwhelmed by unprecedented sensations – above all, pervasive love, as if wrapped in an eternal hug.

"Welcome to my garden." Anna beckoned her to a bench situated on a patch of lawn.

She sat down next to Anna as if moving in a dream. "There were so many questions I wanted to ask you, but my mind has gone blank."

Anna's face lit with an angelic smile. "You may ask me anything. I think people expect me to be something special because of this." She waved an arm in front of her. "I think they are disappointed when they meet me. I am a simple woman who lives a simple life."

Amy didn't know how to respond. This woman sitting so close to her spoke with the mother of God. She didn't think she was anything *special*? She remained silent letting the experience of visiting the paradise-like garden wash over her. A soul stirring peace filled Amy. In that moment, she realized that any insecurity that she had about playing Anna and doing justice to her amazing life on the screen had disappeared. She was ready to tell the story of a simple woman from a tiny village whom

Mary chose to bring messages of hope to the world.

The rest of the trip passed in a blur. They visited the chapel where Anna had her visions. M.D., PhD., Matt related how he had tried to debunk the supernatural occurrences there starting with landing in jail after accosting Anna with a needle when she was in deep conversation with Our Lady and impervious to any earthly distractions.

"We recently ran through that scene," Brian said grinning at Matt. "Would have been nice if you knew there was no lock on the jail cell from the beginning, right?"

Matt clapped Brian on the back. "She intrigued me from the first moment."

Brian and Matt became fast friends laughing easily together. Amy appreciated MJ's talent in casting Brian in the role. The two men were doppelgangers.

Matt showed them around *Mir* House where Valselo miracles of the roses were confirmed. The camera crew took panoramic footage of the views from Gospa Hill and Salvation Mountain, the meadows of poppies and grazing cattle, and clips of Amy and Brian in various locations in the village in addition to exteriors of the pansion, church, and Anna's house. A full day was devoted to shooting the long hike up and views from Salvation Mountain where Anna saved Matt from a poisonous snakebite. Then the scientist knew with jarring clarity that the miracles of the roses were real, and that Anna *was* conversant with heaven.

Time flew. On board the private jet bound for California, Amy stared out the window committing to memory the terrain that she'd come to love.

"There is something special about Valselo," MJ

said. "It gets under your skin."

"Exactly. I'm already trying to figure out how and when I could come back. I've never met anyone like Anna. Be honest with me, MJ. Do you think I'm good enough to portray Anna's goodness and peace on film?"

Amy's stomach clenched when MJ fumbled with her phone rather than answering her question.

"Um…did you hear me, MJ?"

She held out her phone to Amy, still tight-lipped.

Amy knit her brow and focused on the photo MJ had opened on her screen.

"I took that picture when you were sitting by yourself in Anna's garden. Look at your face," MJ said. "Now swipe to the next picture. That's Anna sitting in the exact same spot. She seems to have a light glowing around her. Go back and really study your picture, Amy. I got a chill when I saw it the first time. You have the same glow. I don't have a single doubt in my mind that you are meant to play this role."

Amy swiped back and forth between the photos, grateful for MJ's powerful affirmation. "Thank you," she said softly handing the phone back. "I needed to hear you say you trusted me."

"I do." MJ narrowed her eyes. "Now I want to know why you're wearing my Nana's cross. Last time I saw it, she gave it to Mike for safe keeping."

MJ burst out laughing. "You should see your face! I've known for years that you were in love with my brother. Has he finally realized you're the one for him?"

Chapter 14

Amy climbed the three ladder-like steps and opened the trailer door bristling with anticipation that first day of shooting. Blocking on set that morning had gone smoothly and MJ seemed more at ease that the problem ridden project might have taken a turn for the better. She drew in a breath at the compact but lavish interior of her "dressing room" and relaxation haven between takes.

Leaving the door ajar, Amy strolled around inspecting the kitchen equipment where she could but wouldn't prepare full meals; a dining table for four; a mirrored, vanity table; two leather, recliner chairs; a large screen TV; and a sprawling sofa, which she discovered folded out into a king-sized bed.

A huge bouquet of red roses, easily three dozen stems, in a crystal vase on the table drew her over to read the card. *Do you believe florists in CA don't carry Lily of the Valley for my girl? These will have to do...pretend I'm there handing them to you and telling you to break a leg. Love, Mike*

She heaved a sigh. "I wish I didn't have to pretend, Mike." Amy inhaled the sweet floral scent and then continued to explore the trailer.

Several framed photos of Valselo landscapes and a picture of Amy, as Anna, and Brian, as Matt, atop Salvation Mountain lined the wall. MJ had even thought to place an eight by ten framed photo of Amy and Mike together at her *Grease* wrap party on a lamp table next to the sofa. Amy had no idea who had snapped the photo catching them both unaware. She couldn't remember when she had looked so radiant and joyful in a photograph.

Amy picked up the picture and gazed wistfully at Mike's smiling image. He didn't beam like that often, but when he did, a dimple appeared in his right cheek and his black-lashed, round blue-gray eyes danced with contagious happiness. He looked like he might burst unless he grabbed hold of her and swept her into a hug or twirled her around in a circle. How Amy wished he could dole out one of his melt-into-his-strong-arms hugs to her in that moment.

"Does everything meet with your approval?"

Amy gave a start. She set the photo back down and spun around to face MJ who stood in the doorway toting a giant, cellophane wrapped gift basket in her arms.

"Are you kidding? This place is amazing. Thank you so much for making it feel so personal." Amy pointed to the wall hangings.

"Gotta keep the talent happy." MJ trundled forward and plopped the basket down on the other half of the dining table next to Mike's flowers. "Phew, this thing is heavy."

"What is it?" Amy stepped to the table for a closer look. "Wow! This is decadent! Is this from you?"

MJ loosened the ribbon which gathered the cellophane on top of the basket until the wrap unfolded revealing the brimming goodies. "Nope. Our mothers apparently got together on this."

Amy plucked out a Mounds bar, ripped open the paper and bit off half of one of the chocolate-covered coconut bars in the package. "Mm. My favorite."

MJ opened a bag of Pirates Booty and stuffed a handful of kernels in her mouth. "Or is *this* your favorite?" she mumbled around a mouthful of food.

Amy riffled through the basket scarfing down the rest of the candy bar. "Oh my gosh, chips, cupcakes, jelly beans, chocolate covered malt balls, *every* kind of M&M's, chocolate covered raisins, cherry licorice, mints, chocolate chews, taffy, animal crackers, pretzels…last but not least, toaster breakfast tarts!"

"Of course." MJ said tearing into a bag of Caramel M&M's. "We need to eat a balanced breakfast."

"What, no cookies or pie?" Amy said.

"Don't our mothers know us *at all?*" MJ shuffled bags around on the table. She ripped open a package of cream filled sponge cakes and bit off half of one, cream oozing from the opposite end. "Makes my teeth ache just thinking about all the sugar we consumed when we were kids. We must have made our dentists rich with baby teeth cavities."

They burst out laughing.

Amy took a seat at the table. "I really am starving. Maybe something salty. You can't beat cheese crackers."

Their moms had provided doubles of each snack food harking back to when they were kids and war might break out over a solo bag of candy.

"I'm with you there," MJ said grabbing her own bag of crackers and plopping down onto a chair across from Amy.

"So," MJ said, chewing on snack food, "is the florist shoppe from Mike?"

"Uh huh. Aren't they beautiful?"

"Sure are. It's not like him to spring for expensive

flowers. I'm impressed."

"No? What *is* like him? Have you met any of the women he's dated? Has he ever been serious about anyone?"

"No and I don't think so. He's never mentioned anyone."

"Really? Huh."

"Why does that surprise you? You've never been serious about anyone either."

"I…" Amy bit back the protest mulling over MJ's statement.

"I guess you're right," she admitted.

"Mike has always been more than just a big brother to me. He was a rock for me growing up and into adulthood. After Dad died, through every breakup and heartbreak and all my career insecurities, he was my shoulder and favorite counselor. But he's *never* given me a chance to reciprocate with him. He keeps his personal life and feelings strictly to himself while drawing me out with ease. I'm positive that he's an ace interrogator."

Amy nodded agreement. Joy flooded her listening to MJ describe him as closed and sort of stingy in spirit. He was the opposite with Amy which made her feel beyond special.

"How are things with you and Ry?"

MJ's cheeks reddened as a Cheshire grin crinkled the corners of her eyes. "OK."

Amy burst out laughing. "Just *OK*? The expression on your face tells me otherwise."

"Can't snow you." MJ patted Amy's hand. "Things are great. Kind of fantastic. I'm afraid by saying that I'm jinxing it."

"Nah," Amy said. "Just go with fantastic."

Amy picked out a couple of square crackers from the bag and popped them into her mouth. Gazing around the trailer, she said, "This place really is luxurious. I feel like a celebrity."

"On this set you are *the* celebrity. However, even though you're the star, Brian has an identical trailer at his disposal. His agent was all over how it should be stocked, too."

Amy snorted. "Yeah, but does he have Cadbury eggs? I think not."

MJ blew a raspberry into her cupped palm. "Good point."

"I've never done the diva thing through my agent." Amy huffed a laugh. "Maybe because they'd laugh in my face if I started making demands like I was a big-name actor."

"You're a smash in every role you play. You could absolutely play the diva if you wanted to. Besides, if I do my job right and give you what you deserve as your director, you can pick any role you want after this."

"From your mouth to God's ears."

Wouldn't that be amazing? Each day apart, she missed Mike with mounting intensity. What if she could choose projects that *only* filmed or were staged in Chicago?

Amy continued to survey her surroundings appreciating the expensive lamps, gleaming appliances, and what looked like silk wallpaper. "Seriously, MJ. You can afford movie star digs for your first project? I would imagine the Valselo trip alone cost a fortune."

MJ kicked back in her seat propping her feet up on the chair next to her. "Honestly, budget has been the least of my worries from the start. Nicole has been very generous backing the project."

"How exactly does all that work?"

"What do you mean?"

"The money stuff. Is Nicole your boss? Do you have to answer to her for everything you do?"

"Not exactly." MJ popped up from the table. "I'm thirsty. Can I get you something to drink?"

"Sure. What do we have?"

"Let's see," MJ hung over the refrigerator door. "Bottled water, flat and sparkling; champagne; assorted fruit juices; smoothies; beer; red and white wine. I think that's it, unless you want me to bring in sodas like Coke and Sprite, etc."

"Geez. Flat water is fine."

MJ strode over to the table and handed Amy a bottle of water. She unscrewed the cap from her bottle and took a swig. "So, Nicole and how this works," she said as she sat down and propped up her feet again on a chair.

"Nicole is the executive producer for the project. Did you ever see the credits role after a movie?"

"Sure. There's a bunch of production companies and producers usually."

"Yep. In our case Nicole offered to back the production entirely when Trey passed on the project. Now, how she does that, maybe through other investors or her father's involvement, I'm not sure. But she's promised to give me sole discretion in Directing the movie. I'm also in charge of production – editing, etc. I've only worked with her husband, Trey, and always as an underling, so I'm not sure about her management style. But Nicole's allowed me to cast all the roles without any interference and has been a dream so far regarding our production budget."

"Did I hear my name?" came from the open doorway.

MJ jumped to attention. "Nicole...hi."

A statuesque, Baywatch busty, platinum blonde breezed inside. A wiry, hawk-nosed man with salt and pepper hair followed closely at her heels. Although the man carried himself with a haughty swagger, Nicole commanded the room and gave the impression that she dominated every relationship.

"Nicole, Trey, this is Amy Jordan Sullivan, my lead actress," MJ said. "Amy, Nicole and Trey Ross."

Amy rose from the table extending her hand. Smiling she shook his hand first and then Nicole's noting that his wife's grip was twice as strong as Trey's. "I'm pleased to meet you both. MJ has told me so much about you...especially you, Trey." She smiled warmly at the straight-lipped man.

"I'll bet." He ignored the women and swept his gaze around the trailer as if tallying up the cost of each feature.

MJ narrowed her eyes at his obvious rudeness.

"Trey and Mary Jean have worked together for years," Nicole said. "Now it's my turn. Right Mary Jean?"

"Yes. I'm excited."

Nicole clasped both of Amy's hands wearing a delighted expression on her unlined, Hollywood-work-done, flawless face. "And *you*, my dear are perfect for the role of Anna. I've educated myself on your body of work and I'm so happy you were available after Bethany Chambers took another role."

MJ put her hands on her hips and faced Trey. "I've been meaning to ask you about that, Trey."

"Why?" His beady brown eyes flashed, and he

upturned his chin in an arrogant pose. His body language screamed, nobody challenges me, least of all you, Mary Jean. "Not that I need to explain myself to you, but I had a better role to offer her."

"I didn't appreciate your snaking her away; especially when location production was about to begin," MJ held her ground.

"What you do or don't appreciate doesn't concern me in the least," he said. "Besides, you're an…"

Nicole held up one hand while the other remained wrapped around Amy's hand. "Play nice, kids," she interjected.

"We're way past Bethany Chambers, now, aren't we, Amy? I'm thrilled she didn't take the role. Amy is much better suited to carry this project," Nicole said in honeyed tones.

"Thank you, Nicole." Amy gently extracted her hand and pointed at the table. "Would you and Trey like to sit for a while? We have drinks and snacks."

Nicole waved off her offer. "Oh no, thanks. I have a luncheon engagement and Trey has a meeting on the lot. I'll drop by the set now before I leave."

"Want me to come with you?" MJ said.

"No, no. I didn't mean to interrupt your meeting here with Amy. Just wanted to say hello. I know this studio inside and out. I've been playing here since I was little, and Daddy brought me to the office with him. Nice to meet you, Amy."

Directing her gaze on MJ, she said, "I promise I won't be a pest, Mary Jean."

"You could never," MJ said. "You're welcome any time."

"Thank you. I may take you up on that. I'm so

excited about this project." She waltzed out the door.

Without a word Trey fell in line behind her and vanished.

"Whoa," Amy said. "I can't decide who's a bigger piece of work."

MJ chuckled. "Trey is temperamental."

"Ya think?"

"And Nicole? Well, Nicole is silver spoon all the way. Her dad is uber rich. I guess that works to our advantage."

"Yep. And we better get to work."

MJ checked her watch. "Liza should be here in a few minutes to help you with your costume, hair, and makeup. Up next is the scene where Matt sneaks into the rose garden."

"Okay. I want to call Mom and Aunt Kay and thank them for the goodies."

"See you in an hour." MJ marched out the door, all business, and closed it behind her.

Chapter 15

Mike had remained busy enough with casework and overtime shifts since she had left to pretend that immersing himself in the job and living in the home that he loved could compensate for her absence in his life. It didn't come close – even when he had consulted on a Milwaukee serial killer case and his line of investigation had led to the capture of the elusive, soulless murderer.

The success on the job was empty. His home with skyscraper views was empty. Worse – his bed was empty.

He lay on his bed fully clothed except for his work-uniform, navy blue, blazer, with his hands tucked under his head, his elbows flared, staring at the ceiling. He should get up and fix something to eat. Maybe watch the Cubs double-header on TV. He rolled onto his side facing "her" side of the bed and caught a faint whiff of her perfume lingering on the pillowcase he had purposefully neglected to launder.

Missing her cut deep. He rolled rapidly away and off the bed before he buried his head in "Amy's" pillow. No wallowing. They'd figure this out. She was worth it.

He checked his watch, happy for once at the two-hour time difference between him and Amy. She might be free to do a video call with him during a lunch break in her time zone. Mike swiped his cellphone off the bedside table and padded into the living room. He positioned a chair in front of the floor to ceiling windows facing inward to give her a view of the Sears aka Willis Tower behind him when she answered his FaceTime call.

Already his mood had improved anticipating a glimpse of her in the flesh. He settled back in the chair, angled the camera of the phone in front of his face and put the video call through. The blooping staccato of rings sounded.

She picked up almost instantly filling his telephone screen with her lovely face and reducing his image to a thumbnail down in the corner. Her black hair was styled straight and cascading over her shoulders – just the way he liked it best. She wore a white peasant blouse and very little makeup. Just a hint of pink shine on her lips and rosiness on her cheeks. She looked perfect.

"Hey there, beautiful," he said.

"You're not looking so bad yourself. I'm so glad you called. Perfect timing. Let me find somewhere to sit."

The focus on her camera blurred as he "traveled" with her. The video feed steadied as she plopped down into one of those Hollywood style director's chairs.

"Are you at the studio?"

"I am." She reversed her camera lens and scanned from right to left. "There's the set in front of me where we're due to shoot the next scene."

"Really? Looks like a gigantic empty room beyond all that equipment. No props? Decorations or anything? What is the scene about?"

She returned the lens to focus on her face spurring him to grin like an idiot into the camera.

"This whole room will be green screen when the

cameras roll," she said. "*But* what the movie goer will see is a walled rose garden with the fullest, lushest, white roses – Anna's miracle garden."

"Kind of skews my idea of the camera making movie magic."

"A little. Everything's tech now. How is your case going? Still working in Milwaukee?"

"No. We closed the case with an arrest last night."

"Mike, that's wonderful! Your work makes all this," she swept her arm in front of her, "seem totally frivolous."

Her smile lit up his soul. How he wished they were together so that he could do things that made her beam at him like that every day.

"Did your team have a lot to do with capturing the serial killer?" she said.

"Not this time. I consulted alone to the investigative team in Wisconsin. I guess Flynn's profiling chops have rubbed off on me more than I knew."

"Wow! I'm so proud of you."

"Thanks, Ames. So…" *I miss you. I want to jump through the phone and crush you in my arms. I want you here with me. Please come home.* "Are you excited about today? Did you get my flowers?'

She slapped her palm on her forehead. "I meant to call right away but I got hung up meeting the producer. I barely had time to get ready for the scene. Oh, Mike, they're *beautiful*. Thank you so much. I've never received such a gigantic bouquet."

"No problem. I'm glad they came in time. Only the best for my girl. Are you on lunch break now?"

"Yes. MJ has spared no expense with the craft services for the cast and crew. But neither of us is hungry. We stuffed ourselves with snack food from our moms. Did you know about the basket of goodies Mom and Aunt Kay sent us?"

He gave her a crooked grin. "I think heard something about their noodling every sleepover junk food wish list the two of you have ever made."

"They didn't miss a single thing. All that sugar made my teeth ache. Ugh, the thought of food right now makes my stomach pitch."

Even frowning, this woman dazzles me. "I guess it's a little early to know when you might have a break in your production schedule?"

"It is," she said. "Why? Are you able to get time off?"

"Yeah, I think so – especially since I solved the Campus Killer case. Let me know as far in advance as you can, and I'll see if I can juggle my schedule."

"Of course."

"Five minutes, guys." Amy turned her head toward the sound of his sister's voice.

"You've gotta go," he said wishing he could keep the video feed open and just watch her move through her day.

She tilted her head and smiled sweetly. "I do. I'm sorry. If it isn't too late, I'll call you tonight."

"Okay, Ames. Go knock 'em dead."

"Hm. Is that break a leg to a homicide cop?"

Mike chuckled. "Something like that. Miss you."

"I miss you, too."

"We'll talk soon."

"I can't wait."

"Bye, sweetheart."

"Good-bye Mike."

Mike disconnected the call and slumped in the chair. He should follow through on his original plan to make himself something to eat or maybe tune in to the Cubs game. He'd much rather check airfares from Chicago to L.A. and put in for some R&R time off before the inevitable next homicide assignment tied him down. He switched on the TV resolving to reel in the impulse, remain patient and watch the Cubbies lose instead.

****

Amy drifted nearer to where MJ stood going over instructions to the camera crew who beamed at her as though she were delighting them with every word she said. Observing her dearest friend closely, Amy was impressed with MJ's gentle touch yet steady hand giving directions. Amy knew from experience that directors rarely took the time to treat cast and crew with such careful consideration.

MJ's gaze fell on Amy who gave her a little wave.

"Amy, good you're here." She scanned the vicinity. "Brian, there you are. Good. Let's start."

This scene was one of Amy's favorites in Anna Babic's story. Matthew Robbins, the one-hundred percent objective, M.D., Ph.D., had come to Valselo intent on disproving that Anna, and two of her childhood friends, had experienced daily apparitions of Mary of Nazareth for years in the tiny Croatian village where they had lived since birth. His mentor, Harry, had dramatically left his research job working with Matt and established a medical facility in Valselo after his wife, Jenna, believed that she was miraculously healed there.

Matt resolved to discredit Anna and convince Harry to return to his senses and come home to Chicago. However, Matt's tests on Anna raised more questions than answers. During an apparition, Anna didn't respond to high decibel noises, or glaring lights in her eyes, or needle punctures that he administered. She passed a lie detector test with flying colors.

Anna figured prominently in the miraculous healings that medical science couldn't explain. She distributed white roses from her garden to pilgrims. Harry's wife, Jenna, was a recipient of one of Anna's roses. Before her visit to Valselo, her legs were virtually paralyzed. When she got off the airplane after sleeping during the entire international flight home, she was able to walk.

The scene opens just after Jenna refused to allow Matt to test her "Anna's rose." Still perfect and perfumed after years in Jenna's possession, Matt was itching to subject the flower to scientific analysis. Jenna wouldn't part with the rose, her most prized possession. Matt decides to scale Anna's garden wall in the dead of night and steal one of her roses, hellbent on conducting his tests.

Amy took her place on the mark that located her just inside the garden wall and Brian positioned at the center of the set, his back to her, his head hung.

"Lights, please," MJ said.

The three walls around Amy glowed iridescent green. Pale white downlights created puddles of moonlight at Amy's and Brian's feet.

"Good," MJ said. "On three, begin." She held up a hand and raised a finger with each count, "One, two, three."

Anna took a few steps toward Matt and then pulled up short, her arms crossed, staring at his back.

"You don't need to say anything. I shouldn't be

here," he said.

"You're welcome here, Matt. But the gate was locked."

"I scaled the wall."

"Oh! For what reason?"

"To steal a rose."

"Look at me, Matt."

He raised his head and turned around slowly to face Anna.

"You could have asked me. I would…" Amy bit back the rest of her line as Brian doubled over his arms gripping around his stomach.

"Uh…" he groaned holding up a finger. "Give me a…"

A gush of vomit splattered the floor.

"Oh my gosh!" Amy spun around. "We need some help, please."

Her jaw dropped at the sight of the crew behind her doubling over just like Brian. Some raced away presumably to find a rest room. Some didn't make it that far before spewing sickness.

"What the *hell* is going on?" MJ bellowed.

MJ jumped out of the director's chair and spun around. "Bring some basins or something," she directed the medical team.

Paramedics swarmed the set. Brian limped away bolstered by a burly medic who had an emesis basin positioned under his chin. There weren't enough medics to go around. MJ and Amy were seemingly the only ones exempt from whatever was happening.

A possible explanation occurred to them both at the same time.

"Lunch!" MJ. and Amy chorused.

136

MJ rushed to the table, Amy in tow, where Felipe and Leticia, the owners of the company who had prepared the food were boxing Chicago style deep dish pizza, antipasto salad, mozzarella sticks and cheddar cubes – MJ's traditional food choices for the first day of shooting since she had started in the movie business.

"Felipe and Leti, I need to take all those leftovers, please," MJ. said.

Felipe wore a crestfallen expression on his face, his brow knit with worry. "You don't think our food made everybody sick, do you?" he said. "We use only the freshest ingredients. We've never had a problem since we started this business twenty years ago."

"I know," MJ soothed. "But I have to look at everything."

"Sure thing, Miz Lynch. We'll be done in a few minutes."

"Thanks."

MJ tilted her head to the side signaling Amy.

Amy picked up on the cue and followed MJ back over to the now completely cleared set.

MJ plopped down in a chair and Amy sat down next to her.

"I'll have to close down production until we get to the root of this," she said misery ringing in her voice. "What the *hell*?"

A paramedic rushed to MJ's side. "We're taking folks in to the E.R. as a precaution. Our preliminary assessment is garden variety food poisoning. But we want to make sure nothing nastier is going on."

"Sure, sure," MJ said. "I know you'll take good care of them."

"Of course," he spun on his heel and left MJ and

Amy alone.

"Well…" MJ's words trailed off as she heaved a sigh and hung her head in her hands. "I've used that mom-and-pop company a zillion times. I can't believe they've served us tainted food."

"Maybe you should get it tested at a lab," Amy proposed.

"I absolutely intend to."

Chapter 16

Amy jogged around the track on the movie lot in rhythm to the music blaring through her earphones. Lost in the hard beat of Ed Sheeran's latest song, she let her mind wander. She had missed Mike's call last night and arose too early to text before she began her run. Their long-distance relationship took hard work to stay connected – much harder than she had thought when they were together in Chicago contemplating separation. So… she'd work harder. The love of her life was worth overcoming any challenges.

Brian jogged up next to her interrupting her introspection.

Plucking her earbuds out, she smiled at him. "I didn't know you ran," she said as she jogged in place.

He bent over at the waist huffing breaths and wheezing. "Obviously I don't," he gasped.

"Are you feeling okay after the food poisoning or whatever that was?"

"Much better, thanks. That was crazy how many of us got sick. Luckily, enough have recovered to go to work today."

"I'm glad we can keep the project moving. We've had so many delays already on this movie set. Poor MJ."

"You mentioned last week that you wanted to go to Mass here like we did in Valselo. I'm leaving to meet my family at church. Would you like to join us?"

"That would be wonderful. I'd love to meet your family."

"One thing so you know what you're getting yourself into. If the little monsters behave, which is never going to happen, but we like to pretend we're in control anyway; we take them for pancakes after church."

"I'm in. Sounds perfect."

Brian strolled with her back to her trailer.

"I can be ready in fifteen minutes. Okay?" She slipped her iPod out of her pocket and turned it off.

"I'll be waiting by the car." He shook his head. "An iPod Amy? Really? Do they even make them anymore?"

"Don't mock it." She playfully punched his arm. "It works perfectly well, and it means a lot to me. My mom gave it to me freshman year and I used it for every cross-country race. I won most of them, too."

He put his hands up in surrender. "I promise I won't say another word about it."

Amy rushed into her trailer. After a quick shower, she twisted her hair into a messy bun on the top of her head, applied a couple of strokes of mascara and a quick dap of lip gloss and hurried back outside.

She found Brian leaning against his car with his head bent over his cellphone. He jumped when Amy tapped his shoulder. "When you said fifteen minutes you meant it."

"Yep. I'm always true to my word."

They pulled into the tiny church's parking lot with a few minutes to spare.

Brian pointed out his wife's car. "Di likes to get here early so we can get the last pew in case we have to make a quick exit."

Amy followed Brian up the steps and entered the dimly lit church.

"Daddy!" A little girl's voice sounded like a gunshot in the quiet space.

Brian leaned down and whispered in Amy's ear, "You can run if you want."

"No way. I want pancakes."

Brian took a seat next to one of two little boys and Amy took the end seat. She smiled as she watched a chubby little girl climb over both boys to wrap her arms around Brian.

"I missed you *so* much, Daddy."

"I missed you too Mabel, but we're in church, so you need to use your whisper voice."

"I love you, Daddy," the little cherub said in the loudest whisper Amy had ever heard. She had to stifle a laugh.

Mabel plopped down on Brian's lap with a loud sigh. Dianne passed down a bottle for Mabel who clasped it and greedily shoved it in her mouth. Sucking for all she was worth, Mabel glanced at Amy, stood up on the seat of the pew with the bottle dangling between her clenched teeth, climbed over Brian and thumped down onto Amy's lap.

Amy was lost in the toddler's wide, blue eyes fringed with impossibly long, lush, black lashes as Mabel stared up at her draining the bottle. Slowly she took the empty out of her mouth and released the biggest burp that reverberated in the church. Amy couldn't control herself and laughed out loud.

Brian's son leaned over his dad, shot Amy a grimace and said, "Whelp, there goes pancakes."

Amy had to keep her hand over her mouth until the

end of Mass to smother the laughter bubbling up inside her. She couldn't even look at Brian because she knew she would lose it.

Freed from the sanctity of the church at last, Amy was still laughing when they scooted into the largest booth at the pancake house. Amy sat next to Brian with his boys, Connor and Liam flanking her other side. Dianne made Connor apologize to Amy for scolding her in church.

The boys ordered pancakes for their guest. They decided on the ones with extra chocolate chips, of course. Perfect.

Amy rolled down her car window and sat quietly gazing outside on the ride back to the studio.

"Too much for you today, Amy?" Brian said.

"Just the opposite. What a lucky man you are. I think I'm ready to start a family of my own."

"Really?" Brian boomed a laugh. "We have friends who think they might be ready to start a family and then after they spend a couple of hours with us, they usually change their minds."

When they arrived at the movie lot, Amy looked at the dashboard clock. 'We have makeup in ten minutes. I'll meet you there."

She hopped out of the car, closed the door, and ducked her head through the open window leaning towards Brian. "Thanks so much for taking me to meet your family. They're awesome."

With only a few minutes to get ready she washed her face, brushed her hair, changed into sweats, and ran out the door, remembering to grab her phone on the way. She had left it charging while she was at church and wanted to touch base with Mike as soon as she could.

Seated in the makeup chair, she was about to call Mike when MJ came in to go over the afternoon's planned schedule. Before they left for the set, Amy sent a quick text to Mike telling him that she couldn't wait to hear his voice and would call after work.

Amy reviewed the script notes for the day while hair and makeup worked on her. The scene opens with Anna walking slowly down the aisle of a chapel reciting the rosary chorused by the pilgrims who gathered there to witness her visitation with the Virgin Mary. Posing as a pilgrim, Matt is poised with his open doctor bag ready to insert needles into Anna's arm while in the thrall of the apparition, believing that he'll get an immediate reaction and prove her a sham.

Amy hit her spot at the back of the chapel waiting for MJ's call.

And action.

Anna travels down the aisle and stops in front of a simple kneeler. In the front row, Matt's hands shake taking a syringe out of his bag and concealing it along the wrist of his right hand. Anna kneels and Matt follows suit with the rest of the congregation. On his knees on the stone floor, Matt tenses for action. Anna's right elbow rests on the front railing of the kneeler, inches to Matt's left. Clad in a white, cotton shirt with three-quarter length sleeves – her exposed forearm is a perfect target.

"Now and at the hour…" Anna stops praying abruptly.

Matt glances left. Her eyes are upturned and fixated on a point on the far wall, her features transformed – angelic - glowing. He rummages in his bag for an alcohol wipe, rips it open and swipes Anna's forearm. Rapidly he slips the prop needle into her arm leaving a droplet of fake blood. No reaction at all from Anna.

He dots more piercings along her arm. Nothing. He pulls a lancet from his bag and snags her right thumb, angled back from her prayer-clasped hands. He jabs at her finger a couple times triggering the retraction mechanism, squints his eyes, stares at her face, and garners no reaction other than a few crimson droplets of engineered blood.

Stirrings behind him. Nothing spoken yet, but he's running out of time. He grabs a larger gauge needle and inserts it in her arm. Angry raised spots multiply from his probing that leak thin red rivulets, pooling into the crook of her arm, and spreading blooms of maroon stains on her immaculate shirt.

Amy broke her pose grimacing. "I'm sorry MJ. I can't keep going. This hurts too much." Tears pooled in Amy's eyes. Blood trickled down her arm on to the floor.

"What do you mean?" Brian stared aghast at the needle in his hand and then dropped it on the floor. "This is actually stabbing you?"

He grabbed a handful of gauze pads out of the medical bag and pressed them along Amy's arm.

MJ ran down the aisle yelling, "Medic! Where's the prop master? Now!"

"What the hell happened here?" She picked one of the syringes up off the floor and examined it. The prop needle should have retracted with pressure leaving a droplet of fake blood on Amy's skin from the syringe reservoir. Repeated use *was* supposed to leave more blood behind for the ultimate effect. But the needle in MJ's hand was sharp and rigid.

"Amy are you okay?" MJ's voice quivered.

"I tried to make it to the end of the scene, but I couldn't hold pose with the pain. I didn't know we were going to use real needles." Tears ran down her cheeks.

"Sorry? You don't have anything to be sorry about. I would never expose you to that. I can't imagine how the equipment in Matt's bag was tampered with. Heads are going to roll."

A nurse bustled quickly to Amy's side and assessed the wounds.

"Does she need to go the hospital?" Brian asked. "I have a car. I can take her. I am *so* sorry, Amy."

"No," the nurse said. "I don't know how sterile the needles are, so we'll give you some antibiotic, Amy, to prevent infection. She calmy cleaned and wrapped the punctures and gave Amy some pain medication. "I'll check on you tomorrow. Get some rest."

"I don't need any rest, MJ," Amy said. "We can finish the scene. I'm ready to go. I'll change my shirt and do a make-up touch up."

"Absolutely not." MJ faced the crew milling around. "We're done for today. Be back here tomorrow morning at nine. Thanks guys."

MJ rubbed a hand over her face. "Why don't you go rest in your trailer, Amy? I'll finish up here and I'll bring pizza over. How does that sound?"

"Are you sure? If you want to keep filming, I can do it."

"No, we'll pick it up fresh tomorrow. Pizza it is and a large bottle of wine."

"That sounds perfect. Brian why don't you join us? You could use a drink, too. You look pale."

All the color had drained out of Brian's face when Amy had stopped the scene. She knew he felt responsible

145

for what had happened.

"Thanks, Amy. I'll walk you to your trailer. I'll come over after I change. I have a couple of bottles of wine in my trailer. I'll bring *all* of them." He gave her a wan smile.

She patted his arm. "I'm okay, Brian. It wasn't your fault."

"Sometimes I think this production is cursed."

"I don't know," she said. "Everything that's happened could have been worse. Maybe someone is watching over us."

Amy wrapped and taped a garbage bag around the bandage on her arm so she could shower leaving the bandages slightly damp but worth it ridding herself of sticky, metallic smelling blood. She put on soft pajamas with a matching robe and settled down on the couch eager to speak with Mike.

Her arm throbbed as she waited for him to pick up the phone, praying that he would.

"Hello," came his clipped greeting.

"Oh Mike. Hi. I've had such a crazy day."

"Yeah, I know. The photos are everywhere."

"Really?" She frowned wondering who on the set might want to publicize today's problems. And why? "Wow. MJ will be pissed that they leaked."

"That's all you can say? MJ will be pissed? What about me? Didn't you think I'd be pissed when I saw them?"

"Why would you be pissed?"

"Brian?"

"What? It wasn't his fault, Mike. Did the photos paint it that way?"

"So, you're admitting it's your fault?"

Amy felt woozy and muddled. "What? How could this possibly be my fault? And, for the record, you don't seem particularly upset about my arm. Did the photos show all the blood?"

"What are you talking about?"

"My injury on the set. You sound so mad at me; and I have no idea why."

"Because photos of you and Brian are splashed everywhere online. The two of you going into a small church this morning and more of you cozy next to him in a restaurant and hanging inside car window – as if you didn't want to let him go."

Her head spun as she slowly digested his attitude and the implications of his behavior. He was jealous in the worst way. Mike continually failed to trust her.

"And you believed that Brian and I are dating? Or whatever?"

"What was I supposed to think? The photos made that obvious; and the headlines were clear."

"Clear, huh?" Anger shot through Amy. "Let me *clear* things up for you. Brian kindly invited me to church with his *family*. I fell in love with his little girl, Mabel and his two boys, too. The whole time that Mabel spontaneously sat on my lap, I daydreamed about us and the family we might be lucky enough to have one day. I couldn't wait to tell you about it. I couldn't wait to tell you that his wife, Dianne is a writer. She's doing a screenplay for a Christmas movie that the Hallmark Channel has picked up for production and she thinks Brian and I would be perfect for the leads in it. But most important to me, I couldn't wait to hear your voice. Clear enough for you?"

"Ames, I'm sorry."

"That's not good enough tonight, Mike. I'm aching physically and emotionally. I'm done justifying to you. Good night…"

"Wait, Ames. Don't go. How were you injured? What's going on there?"

"Not tonight. I have a lot of thinking to do. I'm not sure we can continue—"

"Don't say that, Ames. Of course, we can. I just love you so much…"

"Really? Well, you have a funny way of showing it. You should never have jumped to the conclusion that I would cheat on you. I never would. You're an ass."

Amy disconnected the call on a sob. She buried her head in a couch pillow and let the tears flow.

Her phone immediately rang, but she ignored it and then turned it off without listening to the voicemail message.

Chapter 17

"I'm supposed to ask, no beg, you to please, please, for the love of God, please, call my brother." MJ shrugged her shoulders. "There. Sisterly duty done."

Amy snorted. Of course he'd go through MJ. "Okay. Thanks. Message delivered. Are we ready here?" she said touching Matt's doctor bag lightly.

"Checked and rechecked, and then checked again." MJ closed the bag and grasped the handles tightly in her right hand swinging it off the prop table. "I'm not letting this sucker go until you're all in place and the cameras are rolling."

"Appreciated." Amy ran a hand along the length of her arm, now bandage free and covered with some sort of medicinal makeup to conceal the string of punctures from yesterday's mishap.

"Does your arm hurt too much?"

"Not at all. I'm good. This is such an important part of the movie. I'm excited to enact it. You know, MJ, I'll never be able to thank you enough for this opportunity. I have a passion for this story and it's a privilege to play Anna."

"Gees. After all this, I'd think you'd regret ever signing on."

Amy touched MJ's shoulder. "Not a single regret. I love this work. Let's do this."

"I've reviewed the footage from the shoot yesterday.

We can pick up right before you stopped the action. Amy, the scene is perfect so far."

"Huh! Nothing like reality, right?"

"Yeah, well. Let's ditch the reality from here on in. I'd like my actors in one piece when this thing wraps."

"Can't disagree with that." Amy made to step away from the table.

MJ tugged gently on Amy's shoulder stopping her forward momentum. "Before we start work, do you want to talk about what's going on with you and Mike?"

She grinned at her in response. "Hell no."

"Okay then." MJ walked briskly toward the string of cameras. "Come on people. We're going to finish the scene from yesterday."

Brian shoved a piece of bagel in his mouth, stepped away from the craft services station and drew near Amy. "Good morning. Are you up to this?" he said.

"You bet. The question is, are you? How's that hangover?" Amy said regarding him with amusement.

He had downed a bottle of red wine yesterday all by himself and then topped it off with a couple glasses of Chardonnay. A mean wine hangover was inevitable with all that mixing.

"Makeup and ibuprofen are invaluable inventions."

She giggled. "They are that."

Amy strolled on to the set and took her position on the kneeler. Brian knelt on the floor beside her and upturned his eyes pinning MJ with his gaze as she handed him the medical bag. He fixated first on the bag, and then back up at MJ, his unspoken question instantly apparent.

"Yes, it's safe. Triple checked and never left my possession. Makeup!" she yelled.

MJ directed the artist to recreate the blood ooze and needle prick damage to Amy's arm from the day before. They'd pick up the action from where Matt jabs Anna with the last largest gauge needle. Pandemonium would break out among the pilgrims in the chapel and lead to Matt's imprisonment at the conclusion of the take.

The leads and ensemble pilgrim gathering made quick work of enacting the remainder of the scene. MJ was thrilled at the easy one take, and she dismissed the extras for the day casting sunny smiles all around…until Trey appeared in their midst like a specter materializing straight off a country club tennis court.

"Um…Trey," MJ sputtered as Amy and Brian instinctively closed ranks around her. "I had no idea you'd be on set today. Where's Nicole? Can I help you with something?"

"Nicole's doing whatever it is she does with herself all day. I thought I'd help you with your little project. Truth is," he tilted his head back, narrowed his eyes and gazed around as if looking through a pair of bifocals, "I feel a little guilty leaving you adrift."

Color rose in MJ's fair skin. "Adrift? What the…"

Amy faced Trey squarely, fisted her hands and rested them on her hips. "MJ is far from *adrift*. I've yet to work with a better director."

"I'll second that," Brian boomed.

"Well, that's nice," Trey said with just enough snide undertone to convey just how unimpressed he remained. "But the student can always learn a little something from the master. So, indulge me, Mary Jean. You'll thank me at the end of the day."

He turned his back on MJ, Brian and Amy and strolled the perimeter of the set. "What's next on today's schedule? I can't say I'm familiar with your script, but if you give me a scene synopsis, I can work with that."

Brian tilted his head toward MJ's ear. "Can't you get rid of this asshole?" he said through clenched teeth.

MJ scrubbed her brow with her hand. "Maybe not right this minute. Because of Nicole's backing I'm not sure what role Trey plays in all this. But I'll be one hundred percent sure after I have a long conversation with his wife later. For now, you just do what you do best, and I'll deal with him."

"Whatever you want, MJ," Amy said. "Are we doing the snake poisoning scene on Salvation Mountain next per the schedule?"

"Trey or no Trey, no reason not to."

"Gotcha," Brian said. "I'll get into hiking gear costume." He winked at Amy. "Get ready to save me, Anna. I've got little kids at home."

Amy chuckled and then sought out a quiet corner where she could regroup before she was called to the scene. She needed some distance from the obvious frustration MJ was suffering trailing Trey and buffering her cast and crew from his overbearing personality. She needed distance from her jumbled feelings for Mike, too.

The downside of her career would always include exaggerated headlines and fake news about her personal life. The camera bugs had "papped" her so many times before that she no longer paid attention to how skewed those photos of her were presented to the public or what crazy things were said about her so-called romantic entanglements in the popular media. But Mike had no experience with all that and she truly wanted to cut him a break. How could he sift through all that trash alone in Chicago while the media portrayed her as merrily living the single Hollywood life without him?

But he should know in his heart that she would never betray their love. He was a skilled interrogator. Couldn't he tell fact from fiction?

She longed for a future with him – a future that held everything possible for them: love, adventure, family, *and* career. Amy was willing to accept the danger and crazy hours that Mike's career entailed because she'd never expect him to sacrifice doing what he loved for her sake. Granted, his line of work would never involve far-fetched reports of his fictitious affairs, but hers did and would. He'd either learn to live with that or they couldn't continue in any relationship, long distance or otherwise.

Seated on the outskirts of the set, Amy observed the interaction unfolding between Trey and MJ. Trey had insinuated himself next to MJ as she checked the equipment, with her clipboard in hand, and gave direction to the camera crew and grips. Lights flared on, off, changed color and then repeated as she choreographed their use. MJ rarely raised her voice and then was no exception. Amy couldn't hear a word that she said, but she knew her directions were given gently but firmly and usually with a big dose of humor. With Trey shadowing MJ, her best friend's calm demeanor was forced. Amy was sure that no one knew it but her.

Amy rose from her seat and drifted toward the set readying for her cue to enter the scene. Matt had "scaled" the mountain and was seated on a plateau taking in the imaginary vista from his perch in front of the green screen.

Trey's nasal voice sounded. "Cut!"

MJ bolted upright squaring off in front of Trey's chair. "Trey. You. Will. Refrain. From ever. Ever. Doing that again on my set."

"You should—"

"I'm not interested in what you think I should or shouldn't do while we're filming." MJ's tone cut razor sharp.

"I respect you, Trey and always will," she said firmly. "But if you can't act like a guest during active filming – which you *are* here. Then I need you to leave."

The entire cast and crew erupted in resounding applause.

MJ bit back a grin. "Understood?"

The man shifted in his seat and grumbled. "Fine. Do it your way."

MJ turned away from Trey and focused on her lead actor. "Ready, Brian?"

"Ready."

"All right, action."

Matt scrambled upright and began the descent through the brush off the path when the asp struck. He gasped and fell to the ground clutching his leg.

MJ called for a break in the action and strode briskly toward Wayne, the boom operator. She said a few words to him out of Amy's earshot and then he vacated his seat so that MJ could presumably indicate the angle she wanted to go for in the scene. Wayne smiled and nodded agreement after MJ's demonstration. She returned to her chair next to Trey, who unexpectedly and thankfully had remained mum and seated during her exchange with the boom operator.

"Okay, Brian. We're rolling on three." MJ held up her right hand extending three fingers.

Brian assumed Matt's prone position on the craggy terrain rocking in agony from the snakebite. Amy stood

154

outside the reach of the cameras' lenses ready to climb to Matt and change the course of the character's life with a miracle rose.

Anna scrambled up a pile of rocks to the rough ground where Matt lay unconscious. Clutching a full-bloomed, white rose in her hand, her facial expressions and body language conveyed that Matt's imminent danger terrified her. Known for acting as an instrument of miraculous healing, could Anna heal the man who meant everything to her?

Amy sensed the motion of the boom moving in for the "aerial" angle in her peripheral vision. In the next instant, a resounding crack sounded as if lightning had struck the building. Horrified, Amy watched the boom completely collapse. Metal crashed to the floor with a sickening squealing sound and Wayne was crushed to the ground in a heap.

"Dear God!" MJ screamed. "Help him!"

Paramedics, cast, and crew rushed to Wayne who lay scarily inert on the floor. In minutes yet another casualty of the filming of *Rose of the Adriatic* was carried off the set on a stretcher bound for the hospital.

Amy stood frozen to the spot helplessly watching the accident transpire. MJ frantically raced alongside the stretcher and out of sight.

Brian came up from behind her and wrapped an arm around her shoulder. "Now do you believe this production is cursed?" he said.

She shivered. "I don't know. Maybe."

"What should we do?"

"I guess wait in our trailers for word from MJ?"

"Yeah. I think that's what she'd want."

"Do you think Wayne will be all right?"

"I pray he will. It all happened so fast, I'm not sure how seriously he might be injured."

"Right. Okay. We'll pray for him."

"Of course. I'll head to my trailer. Text me if you hear anything from MJ and I'll do the same?"

"Sure. See you later."

Amy's heart thundered in her chest. It wasn't lost on her that just minutes before, MJ had taken the cameraman's place on the faulty boom. Neither was the fact that Trey had yet to move from a relaxed position on a director's chair.

Chapter 18

The nightmare bolted Amy awake. She darted her eyes around the room, disoriented and panicky. The sight of the familiar seafoam-colored walls and sheer curtains billowing in the breeze calmed her pounding heart. *Home.*

She stretched her arms overhead and yawned, thankful that the dream that shook her to the core was not her reality. Amy was there in her bed, not running after Mike after he had told her that he wanted nothing to do with her. Her heart had cracked at the loss.

Their conversation the night before had mended the rift that the photos of her and Brian had torn open between them, hadn't it? Was their love so fragile that her dream was prophetic, and Mike would never fully trust her?

A text notification sounded on her phone. Reading the message, she smiled; all vestiges of the nightmare wiped away. *Good morning, beautiful. I hope you have a great day. I'm off to work. Will talk to you later. Your Mike*

My Mike. What a perfect way to start the day of nesting at home with no schedules or filming setbacks plaguing her.

Last night she had towed MJ away from Wayne's bedside. He would fully recover from a broken leg – a minor injury considering how much more extensively the boom collapse might have harmed him. He was surrounded by his wife and three doting daughters when Amy nudged MJ out of his hospital room.

Amy had cajoled MJ into handing over her car keys and then chauffeured her with the radio blasting to Amy's secluded home in the Hollywood Hills. MJ had already decided to cancel further work on the film for the remainder of the week and had no problem turning her phone off as they approached the gate at the end of the winding drive up to her house. She hoped that a little therapeutic R&R would eliminate the dark circles under MJ's eyes and banish worries – at least temporarily.

She fixed an abundant breakfast for her and MJ gazing out the window as she worked. The unique design of the house afforded total privacy to the roommates. There were two apartment-sized bedroom suites on each of the first two floors. The penthouse floor had an open plan with a modern kitchen, a sprawling living area with two large sectionals and a seventy-inch wall mounted TV, and a dining table seating twelve. A laundry room, a powder room, and a fully equipped gym were built over the four-car garage. The entire back wall of the house was glass showcasing the panorama of the valley below and a sweeping view of the Pacific Ocean beyond land's end.

Footfalls sounded on the stairway and MJ appeared in the kitchen, tousle-haired and still wearing pajamas.

"Good morning or should I say, good afternoon sleepy head," Amy teased MJ.

"I can't believe I slept so late. I'm sorry, Amy."

"Don't apologize. You needed it and I am glad I convinced you to get away for a few days."

"Convinced?" MJ hooted a laugh.

"OK. I'm glad I strong-armed you away from the studio for a few days. You needed to step back for a long minute. Let's fill our plates and take them outside. Look at this picture-perfect day."

Seated at a glass table on cushioned, white wicker chairs, Amy and MJ ignored the food on the plates in front of them transfixed by the breathtaking vista from the balcony.

"This is the life." MJ closed her eyes and breathed deeply.

"I pinch myself sometimes. It's hard to believe that this is my home." Amy speared a piece of pineapple with her fork and popped it in her mouth.

MJ tore off a piece of a flaky croissant and ate it; bit off another piece, practically stuffing the whole thing in her mouth; and then chewed the pastry, her cheeks bulging. She swallowed with a gulp and chased it down with a swig of orange juice. "I didn't realize I was starving until I started eating. Thank you for this."

"Of course. Try the omelet. You need the protein."

MJ grinned at her and dug in. Her plate was clean in minutes. She leaned back in her chair.

"Now that you're rested and fed, can we talk business for just a few minutes?" Amy said.

"Sure. I'm having work withdrawal anyway this morning. Shoot."

"What the heck was Trey's problem yesterday? He acted like such an asshole. You were calm and contained even though he treated you like an underling on your own set. I wanted to slap him."

MJ took a long sip out of her water bottle before responding. "To be honest I wanted to slap him, too.

He's a very demanding man and hard to work for. He doesn't accept mediocre. You've seen his films. He's a genius and I owe my career to him. I think he's having a tough time letting me go. You've probably noticed he has a gigantic ego."

"Hell yeah. But…is it more than business with him?"

"If you mean anything romantic or sexual, the answer is no."

"Did he *want* anything to happen between you? The gossip columns have claimed for years that he screws around with virtually all his protégées."

"Oh, I know about the rumors firsthand. For a couple of months, we were on the cover of every rag in this town when we worked closely together on the movie, *Fill the Stadium*. It was hell for my personal life that's for sure, but I learned so much from him. I wouldn't change one thing."

"So, you don't think the rumors about other women are true?"

"I wouldn't go that far. There was something with an assistant right before we started shooting *Fill the Stadium*. I didn't know her well, but she seemed competent at her job, and there definitely was a vibe between them. We had a break for the Christmas holiday and when we came back, she was gone. No one talked about her. She simply vanished with no explanation from Trey. About a year later, I heard that she had moved to Hawaii, bought a beautiful condominium, and far as anybody knew wasn't working at all."

"That sounds fishy."

"And that's not the only time something like that happened according to rumors. But he was all business and very professional during every project I worked on with him."

"He never hinted that he wanted more from you?"

MJ's expression grew pensive. She nodded. "I remember one time we were all out for a couple of drinks close to the end of production. He got a little too touchy feely for me. You think when that happens you will stand up for yourself, but he was my boss, and I really liked my job." MJ sighed. "I'm embarrassed, but I let him kiss me. Then I went to the restroom and called an Uber. I never went out for drinks with the crew again. He took the hint and never tried anything at all since then." She took another sip of water. "I never told anyone that before."

"Thank you for trusting me with the confidence," Amy said. "Was it hard to work with him after that night?"

"Strangely, it was easier, as if we had cleared the air and moved on. He became a friend."

"Do you think Trey is behind all the problems you're having with the production?"

MJ wagged her head. "Of course not; why would you even ask?"

"He wouldn't help you fund the production, for one, and he also lured your lead actress away at a critical time."

"He never said it, but I think he might have asked Nicole to fund the production. And I'm sure he didn't hold a gun to Bethany's head to take a role in his next blockbuster. Would you leave a production if someone came and offered you a better role even though you had made a commitment?"

MJ paused.

"You don't even have to answer. I know you. You wouldn't."

"True," Amy said. "I just want you to be careful. When the boom came crashing down and everyone was running around trying to help Wayne, Trey sat in the director's chair with a smirk on his face. He never moved."

"I can't believe that Trey could hurt anyone. Is he possessive and would he have been happier if I stayed under his wing on his productions? Yes. I'll admit to that. But he would never want to hurt me."

Amy regretted causing the pained expression on MJ's face. "I'm sorry I brought it up. Trey was probably just in shock like the rest of us when Wayne crashed to the ground. Enough talk about work. Let's get changed and go for a hike, then some pool time and then early jammies. How does that sound?"

"It sounds perfect."

Amy relished the hot-as-she-could-stand-it shower sprays pounding her body. Her unused muscles ached from hiking the steep hills. The hot water worked its magic. The smell of popcorn had Amy's stomach growling as she donned soft fleece pajamas. She piled her wet hair on top of her head with a scrunchie and slipped fuzzy slippers on her feet.

MJ had set snacks out on the coffee table: cheese and crackers, a jar of M&Ms and a huge bowl of fresh popcorn. Amy joined her on the sectional in front of the large screen television.

"I feel like we've time-traveled back to age fifteen at your mom's house." MJ aimed the remote control at the TV, and the sound of Bella Swan's voice filled the room.

In unison Amy and MJ recited along with the actress, "I've never given much thought to how I would die."

"Never gets old," Amy said.

Their favorite tween movie ended with Bella and Edward dancing at the prom. Amy sighed as she rose from her seat and began clearing the table. "Hands down, this is still my favorite end to any movie."

"Only because you're team Edward. No one on Team Jacob likes that ending."

"We never fought with each other growing up until we squared off on those opposing teams." Amy smiled at MJ.

"Ah the good old days when life was so much easier," MJ said as she loaded the dishwasher.

"I'm sorry things are rough for you right now. But trust me things will get better." Amy gave MJ a hug.

"I know they will. Thanks for today. I really needed the escape."

Side by side, Amy and MJ descended the stairs towards their bedrooms.

MJ's phone rang just as she reached her suite's level. She answered, "Team Ryder," as she slipped into her room and closed the door.

Amy's phone trilled at that moment, and she took the call. "Team Mike," she said loudly enough for muffled giggles to sound behind MJ's bedroom door.

"Please don't tell me you guys watched that stupid movie again," Mike's voice boomed in her ear.

"We watched that *amazing* movie again. And before you say another word about our obsessions, your sister needed an escape today and what better way than to watch the greatest movie of all time?"

Amy drifted down the stairs toward her bedroom door, her phone to her ear. "Oh, and by the way, hi Amy how are you? How was your day?"

Mike laughed and took the hint. "Hi Amy. How are you? And how was your day? Ames, it is so good to hear your voice. I miss you."

"Oh, I miss you too. So much."

"What's up with MJ? What did she need to escape?"

Amy spent the next half hour relating all the mishaps on the set ending with Wayne's injury.

"And she didn't think to call me and tell me about any of these sabotages?" He raised his voice.

"What could you have done from Chicago? She didn't want to worry you."

"And you think this guy Trey could be behind this?"

"I can't really say. The way he talked to her and the way he sat there after Wayne got hurt doing nothing to help and appearing totally unaffected stopped me cold. I talked to MJ about him this morning. She doesn't believe that he could hurt anyone – especially her. She still feels he's a friend. I think bringing her here for a few days will help. We had a wonderful time today and tomorrow will just be a repeat. And yes, before you even ask, we'll watch the next movie in the series so that MJ can ogle Jacob all she wants."

"God, I wish I was there despite the dumb Twilight Saga."

"Really? I didn't know you were team Jacob."

"Very funny. You know what I mean."

"I wish you were here, too, Mike."

"When do you think you'll be able to come home to Chicago?"

"I really don't know. If production keeps getting delayed, I don't think anyone is going to get a break until it's finished. You're always welcome here."

"I'll figure out a way."

"That would be wonderful." Amy glanced at the clock. "I didn't realize how late it was there. You really should get to bed."

"Thanks for taking care of my sister."

"She's my sister, too. We'll talk tomorrow. I miss you, Mike."

"Good thing you won't have to miss me much longer. Could you open this gate for me, please?"

"What...do you mean?"

"The electronic gate fronting your house. I like the security, by the way."

Elation bloomed inside her as she flew to the control panel outside her bedroom door to open the gate. She flung open the front door blinking as headlights approached and then switched off.

165

Chapter 19

He had just emerged from the rental car when she barreled into his arms. Mike squeezed Amy tight and buried his nose in the crown of her shampoo fragrant hair. She molded her body to his - a soft bundle in her goofy, puffy pajamas and fuzzy slippers.

She arched her neck and gazed up at him. Her eyes and hair gleamed in the moonlight as if she emitted illumination. The sight of her certainly lit Mike up.

"Nothing feels better than being in your arms, Mike. Whatever possessed you to just drop everything and come to me?"

"This," he said. Mike cupped her face with his hands and kissed her soft lips.

They hung in the increasingly steamy connection. She glued her lips to his with equal urgency as if she had starved for him as much as he had for her. He ended the kiss to catch his breath. Amy panted softly swaying within his arms' cradle. He swooped her up into a fireman's carry and headed toward the entryway of her house. She sighed and nestled her head against his shoulder and then trailed kisses up along his neck stoking the desire he could barely contain during the long travel day to *finally* be with her.

"I hope your bedroom is close. And doesn't involve stairs," he said kicking the front door closed with his boot.

"Yes, it is, and no it doesn't." She pointed to double doors off the impressive two-story foyer. "Through there."

He steered inside her bedroom – an enormous, tastefully decorated room by his standards, fit for a shining star like Amy. The air was redolent with her garden-fresh perfume. Mike couldn't wait to immerse in their intimate connection. He placed her gently down seated at the edge of the bed and stripped off his shirt in one swift motion.

She laid a soft hand over his heart, her warmth radiating on his bare chest. "Excuse me. I'll only be a few minutes."

"Of course."

Amy disappeared behind her bathroom door. Mike took a seat on a bench in front of the king-sized, four poster bed and took of his boots and socks. Lazily rising, he unbuttoned his jeans and unzipped his fly, dropping the pants to the floor and then picking them up to fold neatly on the ottoman of a double-wide chaise lounge in front of a fireplace in a cozy corner of her room.

Still wearing his briefs, he turned down the covers on her bed and slid in between cool, silken sheets. Intending to close his eyes for a few moments, he crashed in the grip of travel exhaustion, instantly asleep.

****

Amy had rushed to add some feminine allure to their reunion: freshly brushed teeth, long mane unbound from the scrunchy and falling loosely around her shoulders, ditched fleecy pajamas in favor of the silk kimono she had hanging on a hook on her bathroom door. And of course, a couple of squirts of perfume.

She opened the door ready to run into Mike's arms,

and then pulled up short at the foot of her bed, a bride without her groom. He lay with a muscular arm stretched overhead, his face relaxed and all boyish innocence in slumber.

"Oh drat," she whispered, smiling. Mike would kick himself in the morning; she knew from experience.

Slipping into bed next to him, she curled up as close as she could to his body without disturbing his sleep.

****

"I think you're drooling, my friend."

MJ's acerbic tone had Amy pulling back from her through-the-window view of Mike's extremely watchable, bathing suit clad body lazing in the sun on her pool deck.

"Um," she said at a loss for where to go next in explaining Mike's presence to his sister.

"Um indeed." MJ was straight-faced and although rare, Amy had no idea what her sister of the heart thought about the unplanned visit.

"Yes, well…" Amy fussed with a leaf of a plant on the windowsill. "As you can see, Mike came to visit us."

She burst out laughing. "I sincerely doubt that Mike is visiting *us.*" MJ plucked an apple from the bowl on the kitchen counter and crunched a bite out of the fruit.

Chewing widely, she took a seat on a bar stool and gazed steadily at Amy. "I'm truly happy for you, Ames. Always. As for my brother – you couldn't find a better man. But don't tell Mike I said…"

"Don't tell Mike what?" He stood leaning against the patio slider doorframe backlit by the sun, a Chicago transplant to California golden boy. His muscular body gleamed with suntan oil.

Amy had a hard time concentrating on anything

other than his sheer physical presence in her kitchen. If MJ weren't sitting right there, she would attack the man.

MJ narrowed her eyes and glared at Mike defiantly. "Don't tell Mike that he's on his own while we spend our mini vacation *exactly* as planned. If you say one word about the Twilight Saga, I'll kill you."

He stepped into the room, slid the door shut behind him, and sauntered over to MJ. He planted a kiss on the top of her head. "Charming, as always sis."

Mike pulled out a chair and straddled it facing Amy and MJ. "I didn't realize I'm interrupting your vacation. *Or* that you're still obsessed with that YA trilogy."

"It's a classic," MJ said breezily.

"Classic wishteroo if you ask me."

"Is not…"

"Is too…"

Amy burst out laughing. "Doesn't matter how old you two are. We need Aunt Kay here to referee."

"For the record, she thinks those movies are wishteroos, too."

"What in heaven is a wishteroo?" Amy said.

MJ and Mike widened their eyes.

"You've been a part of our family since you were ten and you *never* heard that before?" MJ gaped in disbelief at Amy.

Amy wagged her head.

"My dad coined it when we were kids and our family went to the show together," Mike said. "And he never used it except to refer to movies. It means a stinker, a real disappointment."

"Huh. That's kind of catchy."

"Yep. You'll see," MJ said. "When you describe the next bad movie, only the non-word, wishteroo will do…"

169

"As in, you're going to torment me with silly vampire wishteroos *again*," Mike sneered.

Amy drifted over to him and patted his arm. "A small price to pay for our company," she teased.

His gaze locked on Amy, his eyes darkening beneath hooded eyelids. She flushed reading those bedroom eyes.

"I'd pay a very high price for your company," he said, his gaze never wavering.

"Hello," MJ said waving both hands in the air. "I'm right here you two."

Amy chuckled and returned to a more neutral zone behind the counter. "So… can I fix breakfast? MJ what would you like? Mike?"

"I'll just have some of that protein cereal this morning. I can get it, Amy. Mike, would you like some, too? It's good."

"Sure. But I'll get it." Mike shoved away from his chair and walked into the kitchen.

"Bowls?" he said.

"The top cabinet to the right of the sink," Amy directed.

Mike poured two bowls of cereal topped with milk and handed one to his sister. In between bites they decided that a trip to the beach for a jog and to soak up some sun was perfect for Mike's first day in "paradise". He put on hold his original intention to investigate the so-called accidents on the movie set until filming resumed.

For the next two days Amy couldn't remember when she was happier. Relaxed and loaded with energy, she, Mike, and MJ spent their mornings and afternoons hiking, jogging, swimming, and lazing in the abundant sunshine. During the evenings, Amy made good on her promise to MJ to don pajamas and eat finger-food dinners in front of the TV while watching their beloved vampire versus werewolf teen fantasy.

Each evening Mike sat between MJ and Amy on the sectional displaying snarky good nature and providing hilarious commentary, reminiscent of their history together when the Twilight Saga movies first released. Amy's girlhood crush on Mike by then had grown to epic day-dreamy proportions. Now she didn't have to dream about what being with him might be like. Mike shared her bed and their passion for each other seemed endless. The only thing that marred Amy's joyful existence was thinking about how bereft she'd feel when he left after his ten-day leave.

****

MJ was eager to get back to work and didn't want to dally over breakfast the morning that filming was slated to resume. She opted for an insulated cup of coffee on the go and sped out the door the minute that Amy arranged her ride to the studio with Mike.

He wanted to nose around the accident-prone set convinced that none of the incidents were accidents at all. Amy toasted bagels and poured two mugs of coffee for them. Mike downed his breakfast standing side by side with Amy at the kitchen counter and then headed out to his rental car a half hour after MJ's departure.

Amy gave Mike a quick tour of the massive movie lot, her private trailer, and the stage before leaving him at the craft services table to explore on his own while she had her hair and makeup done.

Since the lab results had confirmed that the food on the first day of shooting was laced with powerful emetics, Mike decided to play it safe and gave the fare that morning a wide berth. He watched his sister bustle around with interest – first, as a doting brother who had never seen his sister in action on the job and second, as a seasoned investigator on what he considered a potential crime scene.

A flashy couple approached MJ. The buxom blonde glided several paces ahead of a shorter, hawk-nosed, wiry man. An air of superiority wafted off the duo like a cloud of strong perfume. He thought he detected MJ's sharp intake of breath before she greeted the pair with a smile plastered on her face.

Mike surmised that Trey was in the house. He decided, although uninvited, to insert himself into MJ's business, striding up behind MJ and jutting his right hand toward Trey offering a handshake. His brotherly instincts kicked into overdrive at the hostile expression on Trey's face.

MJ knit her brow stammering, "Um…Nicole, Trey, this is…"

"Detective Michael," Mike interjected hoping MJ would play along. "I'm Ms. Lynch's security consultant," he improvised.

Mike thought it best not to divulge that he was MJ's brother believing he'd appear less a threat to Trey – or whoever was responsible for the acts of sabotage around there.

Nicole grabbed Mike's outstretched hand, scanning his body from crown to boots. "Well, well, Mister Michael, I'm *very* pleased to meet *you*," she said, gazing deeply into his eyes and leaning into the handshake to give him an eyeful of cleavage.

She shifted her piercing gaze to MJ. "Although, this is the first I've heard of hiring a security professional."

MJ arched her brows, her eyes saucers, transmitting the unmistakable plea to Mike to answer to Nicole for her.

He covered Nicole's hand with his left hand drawing her attention. "Oh, I'm not charging Ms. Lynch for my security assessment," he said. "I've been close to the Lynch family since childhood and just happen to be vacationing in California. I volunteered to help Ms. Lynch tighten security after hearing about the recent incidents."

"That's great," Nicole declared. "Isn't that great, Trey, honey?"

"Yeah, whatever," Trey grunted scowling. "Mary Jean, I want to review the lighting for this next scene."

"All right. Why?" MJ said.

Mike wondered if that scowl on Trey's face was permanent. Seemed so.

"Because I said so, that's why." Trey stalked off towards the lighting equipment.

Mike gave MJ a subtle nod hoping she'd understand that he had her back. "I'll let you pros work. I won't get in the way," he said.

"You can get in *my* way any time," Nicole crowed as she plopped down in MJ's director chair.

Mike chose a vantage point a few feet behind Nicole with a view of all possible entrance and exit points.

Amy and Brian emerged onto the set. MJ, with Trey still hanging over her, conferred with her actors briefly and then headed in Mike's direction catching sight of Nicole seated in her chair. She regrouped and sat down next to her without remark. Trey stood apart from the women a few feet in front of Mike's position.

Mike caught Amy's eye. She gifted him with a

sunny smile and once again, he felt like the luckiest man alive.

"OK, guys, we're working on the Jasna fall scene. Where's my Jasna?"

MJ's gaze landed on a sweet-faced woman who raised a hand. She stood next to an identically clad woman with the same stature.

"And your stunt double," MJ said. "Great. Let's get started."

MJ cast her eyes downward swiveling her head back and forth searching the floor beneath the chairs. "Where's my script?" she muttered.

"Jody, have you seen my annotated script?" MJ called out.

"No, I haven't," a pretty brunette responded in motion towards MJ.

"I must have left it in the car." MJ tossed Jody her car keys. "Would you please check?"

Jody caught the key fob on the fly. "Sure. Be right back."

"Amy let's start. Ready everyone? Quiet on the set," MJ said.

Mike couldn't keep his eyes off Amy who had somehow transformed into Anna Babic. She moved differently and her voice changed even beyond her accented English, softer and lower pitched.

A reverberating blast sounded. Mike figured explosive sounds occurred routinely on a movie lot.

"What was that?" Amy broke character. "That was too close to come from another stage, MJ."

Mike was already sprinting towards the exit trusting Amy's instincts. Outside, not far from the stage door, he discovered MJ's car aflame. Metal debris littered the ground and a car door lay on top of charred human remains. The firebomb had surely killed MJ's assistant instantly.

Trey, Nicole, MJ, Amy, and Brian came streaking up behind Mike.

MJ let out a blood curdling shriek. "My God," she screamed. "That's my car! Jody!"

He held out his right arm in front of MJ barring her from rushing further forward. "Don't, sis," he said gently. "Let me handle this."

MJ dissolved in tears. Amy, tears streaming down her face, folded her in her arms. "I've got her, Mike. Oh my God, I can't believe this."

Mike took out his cell phone and called in the homicide setting aside for the moment the stark realization that MJ clearly was the killer's target. He pocketed the phone. "I need to cordon off the area. Is there anything I can use?"

"Luke," Trey barked. "Check in the prop room. I believe there might be some police tape there."

"Thanks," Mike said assessing the expressions on the faces around him. Everyone, including Trey, looked horrified.

Chapter 20

Luke brought Mike several rolls of police tape and helped him cordon off the area around the still burning vehicle. A fire engine, siren shrieking, careened around the corner and braked alongside of MJ's car. An LAFD crew in full gear set to work putting out the fire.

Nicole strode up to Mike, cell phone to her ear. "Good," she said her voice ringing with authority. Gone was the flirty dumb blonde act, replaced by a take-charge boss woman.

She disconnected the call. "I've notified the guards and had them secure the gates to the lot. No one will get in or out, except the coroner and the police. Is there anything else I can do to help?"

"I don't remember asking you to contact security," he said.

"You didn't. I knew who to call; so, I called. My grandfather started this studio. I practically grew up here."

"Thanks. I appreciate your quick thinking."

"My pleasure." She sashayed away and stood next to her husband.

Mike surveyed the area. People had their cell phones out and were taking pictures and videos. Amy had her arm around MJ who looked like she might collapse. Tears streamed unchecked down his sister's face.

"MJ. Why don't you round up your people and get

them back into your sound stage. The police are going to want to question everyone when they get here."

Sirens blared in the distance.

MJ squared her shoulders and shouted out orders to the cast and crew. Relief washed over Mike as his sister took control.

"Let's go Nicole," Trey said yanking on his wife's hand and towing her away from the stage doors.

"Where do you think you're going?" Mike positioned directly in front of the couple.

"I don't have time for this. Get out of my way," Trey barked edging around Mike's rigid stance.

Mike clapped a hand on Trey's shoulder. "You're not going anywhere. Please join everyone inside and wait for the police to arrive."

Trey shrugged off Mike's hand. "Who do you think you are? What gives you the right to tell us what to do?"

"This," Mike held up his badge at Trey's eye level.

"And this," he said opening one side of his blazer displaying his holstered gun, "give me every right. Go inside and sit your ass down."

Trey's face contorted in a scowl. He heaved a loud huff, but silently followed Mike's orders.

A tall, brawny man dressed in the plain-clothes "uniform" of the homicide division familiar to Mike, emerged from an unmarked car that arrived first on the scene. He stood for a moment with his car door open and scanned the area with laser-like focus.

Three police cruisers and a coroner's van pulled in behind him. He moved away from his car and strode over to Mike, his hand outstretched.

"Detective Sam Martinez, and you are?" he said.

"Detective Mike Lynch, Chicago PD." Mike gave

Martinez's hand a shake. "I secured the perimeter. Nicole Ross, one of the studio execs, had security lock down the gates a few minutes ago. No telling if the perp is still on this movie lot. Everybody that was onsite at the at the time of the incident is inside for questioning."

"Thanks for the help. You're far from home, Lynch. What brings you to LA?"

"I'm visiting my sister, Mary Jean. She's directing a film in Stage 7." Mike gave a nod toward the door clearly marked with the number seven.

"She's also the owner of that burning hunk of metal." Mike pointed to what was left of MJ's car.

"Several suspicious, so-called accidents have occurred on this set since my sister started shooting," Mike said. "Also, my girlfriend is starring in the film. I need to figure out what's going on here. Fast."

"Understood. Hang on. I want to get the witness interviews started." Martinez headed towards a group of uniformed cops gathered outside their vehicles and gave his orders.

Mike followed the last man into the stage. MJ had herded personnel away from a cluster of chairs spaced several feet apart in pairs facing each other – makeshift interview rooms. Questioning continued throughout the day. Mike successfully eavesdropped on the conversations while staying out of the interrogators' way. None of the witness testimonies appeared helpful to Mike.

He had texted his Uncle Danny earlier requesting his help with the LAPD brass to pull some strings so he could have an official role in the investigation. He hoped his Police Superintendent uncle could make that happen.

Mike leaned against the doorway leading to the

stage. Martinez walked over to him as the last crew member hurried off into the night.

"I didn't know you were Flynn Dowd's kid," Martinez said.

"I'm not really."

"I just got a call from my boss with orders to include Flynn Dowd's kid on this case. That's not you?"

"Flynn is my stepdad."

"That makes sense. You don't look anything like him."

"You know Flynn?"

"I do. When I was a kid, he worked a case here. Which he solved single handedly. He's the best profiler in the FBI. That's one intense dude. He stayed at my house and my younger brothers were scared to death of him."

"He might seem intimidating, but he's really a quiet, caring man. Why did he stay at your house? Is your dad on the force?"

"Nah. My dad is a teacher. Flynn's sister and my mom were roommates in college."

"That's my Aunt Bridget. She moved back to Ireland to be with their mother. My mom and Flynn visit them every summer. By the way, Flynn's CPD now, not FBI."

"Yep, that came through from my brass." Sam rubbed his hand over his face, yawned and then pulled his wallet out of a back pocket. He took out a card and handed it to Mike.

"It's late. Let's meet at my station house at seven thirty tomorrow morning."

"Sounds good. Thanks." Mike slipped the business card into his pocket.

He waited until Sam's car left the lot and then plodded to Amy's car, exhaustion weighing him down.

A dim light lit Amy's trailer. She lay sound asleep in bed. He tiptoed past without waking her and used the tiny shower to wash away the tension of the day. Clad in gym shorts he drifted to the leather recliner, sat down, and positioned a throw pillow behind his head.

"Don't even think about it." Amy's voice pierced the stillness startling him.

"Come to bed," she said.

"I have never heard three sweeter words." He popped up from the chair and sat on the edge of her bed. "I didn't want to wake you up."

Amy scooted over and Mike eased into bed next to her. She snuggled up against his chest. He drew her closer and traced circles on her back as she nestled her head on his shoulder.

"How are you doing?" Mike said.

"Better now that you're here." She tilted her head and kissed his chin.

"How is MJ?"

"Understandably very shook up. She was here with me until Ryder showed up. He heard about it on the news and immediately chartered a plane."

"How has this already gotten out to the media?"

"You're kidding right? All those cellphone videos? It was probably on TMZ before the coroner even got to the lot. MJ ran into Ryder's arms when he appeared at the door. I'm happy he's here for her."

A tear ran down her cheek. He wiped it away with his thumb. "Aw, don't cry, Ames. I'm here for you. I'll get to the bottom of all this."

"Why Mike? Why would anyone want to hurt MJ?"

"I don't know, but I'll find out. I contacted your dad requesting involvement in the case. He must have talked with Flynn who has a history working with the LAPD. Small world, Flynn knows the lead detective. I'm on the investigative team officially. I have a meeting with the lead detective first thing in the morning."

"MJ said she wants to resume shooting tomorrow if the police let her. I'll have an early start to the day, too."

"I don't see any reason why you can't go back to work – *if* MJ adds a heavy security presence. I'll talk to her before I leave for my meeting in the morning. She needs to close the set and post guards at all studio access points. I'm still concerned about her exposure."

"I know. I'm sure she'll listen to you."

He huffed a laugh. "Have you met my sister?"

Mike stroked Amy's silken hair. "Get some sleep, sweetheart. I'll keep you safe."

Mike wrapped his arms tightly around her intent on holding her all night long. Before long her breathing deepened and she was asleep.

****

Mike tapped his thumb against the steering wheel impatiently. Traffic jams in California were legendary, but the mess surrounding him still surprised him. There was no inclement weather to affect road conditions and no accident ahead, and yet he crawled along in near gridlock.

Good thing he had left the studio earlier than he had thought necessary to arrive early to his meeting. Because at the rate he was moving, it looked like he would just about make it by seven-thirty. His dad had drilled into him an almost military adherence to being on time since he was a kid. He hated to be late.

Mike gave the AI command to dial Flynn's number, disappointed when the call went to voicemail. He left what he considered an impersonal message anyway thanking him for pulling strings on the case with the promise to keep him informed.

Flynn had put up with a lot of teenage combative behavior from Mike when he had dated and married his mom. Yet he was always calm and patient while Mike was being a prick – which was often.

One night had changed their relationship. Mike had gone to a party celebrating the football team's big win after fighting with Flynn over the midnight curfew his stepfather had, in his mind, unfairly imposed on him. Mike had argued that he was too old for a curfew and had ended with the vehement declaration that Flynn wasn't his father and had no right to dictate rules.

Angry from the first moment he had arrived at the party, Mike wound up stupid drunk. So stupid, he had attempted to drive home. His dad was killed by a drunk driver and Mike had never gotten behind the wheel even after drinking just one beer. But not that night.

Fortunately, his friends had confiscated Mike's keys and had texted Flynn. Flynn had picked him up, helped him into bed and had never mentioned that night again.

The next morning his mom had asked Mike to move his car blocking her car in the garage. He had realized that Flynn had somehow brought home his car before his mother knew what a fool he was.

He would never forget Flynn's response when Mike had sheepishly thanked him. "I love your mother and if you died, especially drunk driving, she would die. I can't live without her, and I would do anything to protect her from sorrow."

Everything had changed between them that morning. He understood Flynn's reasoning completely now. He would protect Amy at all costs.

Mike arrived at the station house, early as he originally had intended. He parked his car and sauntered inside the precinct.

He found Martinez hunched over at his desk which was piled high on either side with case files.

"Good morning," Mike said.

Martinez looked up from his work. His eyes were bloodshot. "Good morning. Have a seat."

"You up all night?" Mike sat down on the chair at the side of Martinez's desk.

"I got a couple of hours sleep." He pointed to the coffee maker on the credenza behind him. "Help yourself. It's a fresh pot; I just made it."

"Thanks, I'm good for now."

"These are copies of the witness interviews yesterday." Sam pushed a pile of documents across the desk to Mike. And then he handed him a single sheet of paper.

"What is this list of names?"

"I hate to tell you this, but we might have a conflict of interest with you on the case. Has your sister told you that there have been several problems on different sets in the past?"

"I know about the boom crashing last week on her set and a few problems with equipment being sent to the wrong country. That's about it."

"I have reports of several so-called accidents on the same stage after I did a cross search of our files last night. That's a list of the people who have been present when these accidents occurred."

Mike scanned the document. "It's a long list."

The first name he read was Trey Ross – which came as no surprise to Mike. Then came, Nicole Ross.

He glanced at Martinez. "I don't see a conflict. I met Trey Ross and his wife for the first time yesterday."

"That's not the conflict. The third name on the list is Mary Jean Lynch."

Chapter 21

Mike handed the list back to Martinez. "Yeah, this is personal for me, but I don't see a conflict. MJ worked with Ross before she set out on her own with this movie, so it stands to reason she'd be on the set of his various productions. You can cross her off the suspect list on my word. First: she's incapable of violence. Second: she loves every member of her cast and crew like family. She'd never hurt them. I want to take a hard look at Trey Ross. He's an ego maniac and an overall ass hole. He's been giving my sister a hard time with this movie she's working on from day one. Could be our guy."

Martinez gazed at him steadily before he gave a slight nod of his head. "OK. I'll speak with Mary Jean alone to be thorough and impartial. We can start with questioning Trey Ross together. I'll have my team chase down the whereabouts of the rest of the people on the list and we'll go from there."

"Good. You want to contact Ross to set a time to meet?"

"Nah." Martinez's face brightened with a crooked grin. "Let's surprise the ass hole."

Mike huffed a laugh and scraped back his chair rising to his feet. "Sounds good."

Traffic was sparse along Rodeo Drive. The tony, shuttered storefronts zipped by in a blur as they whizzed past a park sporting the Beverly Hills sign looming over a fountain pool. An ancient, mammoth banyan tree stood sentinel to the famous residential enclave.

"Swimming pools. Movie stars," Mike muttered.

"That and just plain rich out the ass folks."

Martinez steered the car up a steep incline halting at a call box mounted on the side of one of two grey stone pilasters. An intricate wrought iron gate loomed in front of the car, do not enter. The detective rolled down the window and pushed the call button. A strident buzzer blared.

"Yes," came a clipped male voice through the intercom.

"LAPD to see Trey Ross," Martinez said.

"Mister Ross is not at home at present. Regardless, appointments are required for Mister Ross to see anyone…"

"Is Nicole Ross at home?" Martinez interjected.

"Yes, but as I said, you need an appointment."

"Open the gates and advise Missus Ross that we need to see her immediately," Martinez demanded. "I'm conducting a murder investigation and she is a primary witness. That's all the appointment I need to speak with her."

Dead silence.

Martinez drummed his hands on the steering wheel a few beats. "Open the gate now. Otherwise, I'll be back within the hour with a search warrant; and we can do this the hard way."

A metallic click sounded, and the gates parted with an electronic whir in front of the car. Martinez inched forward until the open gap was car sized. He cleared the gate and steered down a verdant path shaded with overhanging tree boughs. The approach to the house was a good five-minute drive.

As Mike had anticipated, the Ross residence was an ostentatious, apartment house sized, gray stone mansion fronted by a circular driveway with a burbling fountain splashing over ornate cherubs as its centerpiece. A showroom of vintage and contemporary luxury convertibles littered the parking apron as if a party was in full swing at eight-thirty AM. Why on earth does anyone need four Ferraris? Heck, Ross fell short of an Italian power car per each day of the week. But he made up for it with two Porsches, an Aston Martin and two Rolls Royces.

The doorbell gonged with gusto and one of the carved wood front doors swung open revealing a straight-lipped man, about six-two, trim, with gelled hair, dressed in a snug cut, blue suit; white formal shirt; and maroon tie. No California cazh for underlings in this household.

"Come in," he greeted them brusquely. "The mistress will meet with you in the solarium. Follow me."

The mistress. Mike found it difficult to attach the prim term, mistress, to the showy, artificially enhanced Nicole Ross.

The "servant" spun a 180 and strode away. Mike and Martinez stepped into the foyer. Martinez lugged shut the front door behind them and they tailed the butler, or majordomo, or whatever his role, through hallways and anterooms painted blinding white. Pollack-like, or who the hell knew, maybe *actual* Pollack canvases, provided smeared vivid color to offset the stark neutrality.

Nicole sat on a white leather loveseat in the glass enclosed room clad in a flowing, flower print caftan. Her blonde hair was clasped back off her face with a banana clip. She wore no makeup and appeared younger, and to Mike prettier, than the woman he had met the day before.

She picked up a coffee cup holding the handle between her thumb and index finger displaying inch long pointed fingernails painted white making Mike marvel at how she could use her hands at all with those stiletto-like encumbrances.

"I take it you want to talk about that explosion yesterday yet *again*," she said, her tone exasperated.

"No, we're satisfied with the testimonies yesterday, although we might need to clarify statements at some point as the investigation unfolds," Martinez said. "We have a few questions about your husband's past productions that may tie in with this investigation."

"All right," she said, her eyes dipping to her lap. "I'm not sure I'll be helpful. I wasn't actively involved with his productions. This movie is the first that I've executive produced."

"We'll be the judge of how helpful anything you might add," Mike said.

To her credit she didn't fidget. She simply nodded.

Martinez dove in. "We have a record of multiple accidents involving injury on the same movie lot in stage number seven, where your husband directed several films. Mary Jean Lynch worked for your husband in all these cases, first in menial capacities and finally as assistant director on his last three films. Do you have any knowledge of these incidents?"

"I know that Trey prefers Stage Seven for various reasons. That's why I chose it for my production."

"We're concerned with the accidents that occurred there. Are you aware of them?" Mike said.

"Some. I know they caused a lot of disruption in

shooting which aggravated Trey no end." She folded the fingers of her right hand over her palm and inspected her nails. "Come to think of it, he was squirrely about it all when I pressed him for details. You see…

"Hmm…" she hedged. "How do I say this without making my husband look terrible, and me look worse for constantly forgiving him."

Mike leaned back in his chair letting Martinez take the lead with questioning.

"We're not concerned with appearances," Martinez said. "We'd appreciate your full cooperation."

"Of course." She averted Martinez's eyes. "Trey has been less than faithful in our marriage, I admit. It took a long time for me to suspect infidelity each time he embarked on a new project. First, his hours were erratic. Kind of the nature of the work. And I didn't question his late night, or even overnight absences because his excuses seemed legitimate to me.

"But…he'd obsessively insist on showering before he'd so much as kiss me hello when he came home. That had my antennae up big time."

"Do you have proof that he was unfaithful?" Martinez said.

"Not concrete. But I started making surprise visits to the sets to observe his interaction with the females working with him. My instincts singled out at least five entanglements."

"Did you confront him with your suspicions?"

"I never got the chance. Shortly after I visited each time, the women I suspected were having affairs with him quit. Problem solved, or at least I thought that."

"Do you know the names of these so-called suspicious women?"

"Yes."

Martinez took a sheet of paper out of his leather portfolio. He handed her a pen and the list he had shown Mike earlier. "Please check off all the names of the women you think were involved with your husband."

She balanced the sheet of paper on her knee and penned check marks rapidly down the list.

"Here." She handed him back the paper.

Martinez scanned the sheet of paper and then continued the questioning. "We'll cross-check the list with injuries reported on the set. Do you know if any of these women were injured before they quit their jobs?"

"No, I don't. Each time when I started to confront Trey by throwing a name in his face, he weaseled out of admitting anything by asserting that this one or that one was a non-issue because she quit. He did tell me about various accidents on the set that disrupted production, but he never identified any of his chickees as injured."

"All right." Martinez trained his eyes on her.

Mike could almost see the wheels turning in his partner's head.

"You mentioned that your grandfather founded the movie studio. Does your family still own it?"

"Yes. My father took over the reins when Grandpa died five years ago."

"Do you or your husband have an ownership stake?"

"No. I stand to inherit the studio, or at Daddy's discretion, take over for him if he chooses to retire. I'm an only child. Trey has enjoyed my influence in backing his productions through my dad. Daddy never says no to me."

"So, Trey is dependent on your wealth."

"Yes and no. He is a wealthy man in his own right

because Trey is a highly talented director with an unwavering intuition for casting. He produces box office smashes; and he is deservedly a multiple award-winning director. But… without my influence on the money side, he would find it much more difficult to do things his way. Nobody in my family, including me, questions his use of financing."

"Huh. Do you use that as leverage in your marriage?"

"I don't know what you mean."

"Do you threaten him that you'll arrange withdrawal of financial backing if he doesn't end his…dalliances with various women?"

She narrowed her blue eyes slightly, her gaze pure steel. "I've never needed to. Although, I would in a New York minute if I'd ever caught him outright. As I said, each suspicion became a closed subject when these women quit."

"You didn't find that in and of itself suspicious? You visit the set, ferret out what you think to be the truth about what's going on, and then mysteriously the problem dissolves without any disruption to your relationship."

She gave him a half smile. "Well, it always struck me as very opportune for him. But why create disruption if problems solve themselves, I always say. I like my life. I'm perfectly willing to ignore his antics if they aren't serious."

"And that doesn't cost you at least some resentment."

Nicole picked at a cuticle. "I didn't say *that*. Of course, I harbor some animosity. But in the scheme of things, what does it matter?"

"Have you been faithful to Trey?" Mike asked.

Her eyes widened with a wicked glint. "Yes, so far. But I could be convinced to stray by a handsome man like you."

Martinez stuffed the list of personnel into his portfolio and rose from his seat abruptly. Mike followed his lead and stood up.

"We've taken up enough of your time, Missus Ross. Thank you for your cooperation," Martinez said.

"Certainly. You gentlemen can show yourselves out? I'd like to stay here and finish my morning coffee."

"Of course." Martinez half-turned to leave and then halted. "You'll make yourself available if we have further questions?"

"Yes. Although I prefer you schedule an appointment in the future."

"We'll try to do that," Martinez said non-committedly.

Mike and Martinez paced out of the solarium, through the immense rooms leading to the foyer and headed toward the entry. The butler materialized in front of them opening the door for their passage with an officious air.

"So, hey," Martinez addressed him. "Do we call you if we want to set an appointment with either of the Rosses?"

"That would be satisfactory." He fished a white card out of his lapel pocket and handed it to Martinez.

"Thanks. We'll be in touch…" Martinez dipped his head squinting at the card, "Giles."

"Very good, sir."

Outside in the balmy warmth and sun glare, Mike and Martinez wended their way back to their car, a drab ugly duckling parked behind the row of multicolored collectible "swan" cars.

"Wow," Martinez said placing both his hands on the steering wheel.

"Swimming pools and rich out the ass folks," Mike quipped.

"She's a major piece of work."

"He's worse," Mike opined. "Can I have that card. I'll call *Giles* right now and set an appointment to question Trey."

"Yeah, do it." Martinez keyed the ignition as Mike dialed the number.

Chapter 22

Mike's foot tapped an audible cadence against the black and white marble floor. He took deep breaths and pushed down the rage threatening to boil over in his chest. He wanted nothing more than to storm out the door released from the eternal waiting room, but he would not give the little weasel the satisfaction. If it took all day; he would wait him out.

Two hours after their scheduled appointment time, Trey Ross breezed past his receptionist's desk and pushed the door to his office open, ignoring Mike's presence. Mike cleared the distance from his chair to the door in two steps stopping Trey from slamming it in his face.

"Come in," Trey barked sarcastically, using his arm to point the way.

Mike stomped to a chair in front of an oversized weathered mahogany desk and sat down. Trey glared at him from behind the giant desk. Mike met Trey's eyes and held his stare observing sweat beading on his subject's forehead as the seconds ticked by.

"I'm a very busy man. What do you want?" He averted his eyes and fiddled with the keyboard of his computer fixating on the monitor pretending Mike wasn't there.

Mike slid a sheet of paper across the desk onto Trey's hand on the keyboard.

"And this is?" Trey said.

"That is a list of the accidents that have occurred in the last two years on the sets of your movies." He slid another paper across the desk. "And that is a list of the people who have been on every set where the accidents happened."

"Accidents happen on all sets, not just mine. I suggest you contact Spielberg and Tarantino and ask them about accidents that have occurred on their sets. And may I point out that I have never had a fatality on any of my sets. Mary Jean Lynch, however, has had numerous accidents and a fatality. Shouldn't you be questioning her?" he said smugly.

Trey glanced down at the list of employees. "And I see her name there on your list. I don't have time for this. I suggest you talk to her."

Trey rose to his feet and made to move away from his desk.

"I suggest you sit your ass back in that chair or you will be taken down to the precinct to answer questions." Mike slid a notebook out of his pocket and referenced the questions he had jotted down while he had twiddled his thumbs waiting for Trey to show up.

Trey eased back down into his seat wearing an expression of open hostility on his face.

"Why do your assistants leave before the film is finished?" Mike said.

"Excuse me? What does this have to do with anything? I thought you were here to question me about the car explosion? Which, by the way, I know nothing about."

Mike disregarded Trey's bluster. "Answer the question. Why do your assistants keep quitting?"

"You'd have to ask them."

"I plan on it, but I would like to hear why you think they leave."

Trey dropped the aggressive attitude and tilted his head to the side as if cooperating with Mike now and thinking hard about his answer. "They want more from me than I can give them. I have to let them go when that becomes an issue."

"What do you mean they want more?" Mike pressed.

"I mean…well, this is uncomfortable. But I mean that they want more than a professional relationship with me."

"You're saying these women are coming on to you and you turn them down?"

"What can I say? I'm a very charming man." He leaned back in his chair his fingers entwined in his lap.

"And married."

"Very happily married," Trey declared.

Mike bit back a response. He picked up the employee list off Trey's desk and handed it to him. He directed Trey to recite each name and comment on his relationship with each person. The paper shook in Trey's trembling hand as he read.

Trey feigned ignorance about more than two thirds of the names listed. "I have assistants who deal with the crew. I have more important things to do on a film."

Mike pressed on, going over the list again, rephrasing his questions, and changing their order hoping to grind Trey down and trip him up.

He stood abruptly having reached the limit with Trey's egotism and evasiveness. "We're done for the day. I'll let you know if I have any more questions for you."

Trey was concealing something, but no matter how Mike had posed the questions, Trey had wormed his way out of giving direct answers. His gut told him that Trey could have set the bomb in MJ's car. He just didn't have any proof. Or a clear motive.

Having gotten nowhere after devoting a half day of work, Mike texted Sam Martinez asking how his interrogations were going and if forensics had come up with anything new in the case. His phone vibrated seconds after the outgoing text. Sam wanted to meet at a small sandwich shop not far from the Studio.

Behind the wheel of Amy's car, he plugged the location into the maps App on his phone. He steered through the security gates, waving to the guard as he passed by.

****

Martinez was waiting in a booth, a menu open in front of him. He nodded at Mike in greeting.

"I'm starving. I missed breakfast this morning to get to the set before your sister started shooting. Do you mind if we order first then talk?" Martinez said.

"Not at all. This place smells amazing."

"The food tastes even better than it smells. I eat here all the time. The father of one of the men on my squad owns it. You can't go wrong with anything you order here." He closed the menu and called over the waitress.

"Hey Sam." A young girl approached the table, already writing on her order pad. "The usual, right? Rare roast beef with grilled onions and horseradish sauce with a large order of fries and ice water."

"Yes, please Shonda." Martinez grinned at the petite African American woman. "I don't know why I even

197

bother to look at the menu."

She turned her attention to Mike. "What can I get for you?"

"I think I'll have the same. It sounds delicious."

"It is. My dad makes the best roast beef in town." She took their menus away and returned with two large glasses of ice water.

Sam waited until they were alone to ask Mike how the interview with Trey went.

"I didn't get much out of him. He says his assistants were coming on to him and he had to let them go to keep his marriage happy. I'll follow up with the women involved after we eat. A couple things stood out about him. He was sweating when I started to question him. And when we started to go over the list of employees that were on each of the sets when an accident occurred, his hand started to shake - a lot. The guy was a nervous wreck. But, going over the list was a dead end with him. He said he has more important work to do on the film than to worry about the crew. He has people who handle that for him. He's a piece of work."

Sam listened to Mike with full attention. Shonda came back with their food and conversation ceased until they finished eating.

"I didn't steer you wrong, did I?" Sam smiled, eyeing Mike's clean plate.

"Nope." Mike popped the last fry into his mouth. "I can't remember the last time I had a better meal. Of course, if you told my mom I said that I would have to deny it."

"Dessert or coffee?" Shonda asked as she cleared the plates. Both men turned down the offer for dessert, opting for coffee.

Sam filled Mike in on some of the calls and interviews he had conducted. "I spoke with three of Ross's assistants who were let go and not one of them had a bad thing to say about him. In fact, it was the opposite. They all blamed the studio for firing them and said that Trey helped them get other jobs with other productions."

"Interesting." Mike pursed his lips wagging his head. "Something is off about this whole thing."

"Agreed. I spoke with your sister this morning and she basically agreed with the assistants." Sam scrubbed his chin with his hand. "I thought for sure Trey was our man, but now I don't know."

Mike grabbed the check folder as soon as Shonda set it on the table.

"What's my share?" Sam said pulling his wallet out of his back pocket.

"I've got this." Mike handed Shonda back the folder and told her to keep the change.

"I'll get the next one," Sam said. "I'm heading back to the precinct.

"I'm going to follow up with the rest of the names on the list then go to the studio. Let's touch base in the morning, OK?"

"Yeah."

****

Mike followed Sam's car out of the parking lot and then turned in the opposite direction. As he drove, he tried a few of the numbers on the list leaving voicemail messages after failing to connect with anyone. He gave up after four strikeouts. He wanted, no needed to see Amy.

Situated in Amy's trailer, Mike finished calling the

remaining names on his list without learning anything new. He spent the remainder of the day into the evening channel surfing the large screen TV waiting for her to finish work.

Finally, Amy and MJ stumbled into the trailer. Mike stood up, and Amy walked right into his arms.

"You look beat," he said tightening his hold on her, enveloped in her sweetness.

"We are, but it's finished. The movie is done! I can't believe it." Amy twisted within his embrace and high fived MJ.

"We should celebrate." Mike opened his arms to MJ, and she went in for a group hug. "Do you want to go out somewhere to celebrate?"

"I just want to shower and go to bed." Amy yawned widely.

"And I have more work to do. I want to work with my Editor to get the rough and director's cuts done as soon as I can," MJ said in motion towards the door. "Nicole is anxious to see the Final Cut."

"Wait up, MJ. I'll walk with you." He kissed Amy on the top of her head. "I'll be back in a little while after I talk with MJ."

"What did you want to talk to me about?" MJ said falling into step beside Mike.

"Trey Ross."

"Nope. I already talked to the detective about him. I'm done talking about him."

"Come on MJ. There's a very good chance that he killed your Assistant gunning for you."

"He didn't."

"How can you be so sure?"

"Because I know him. He wouldn't hurt me. Just

drop it."

"I can't drop it. Someone tried to kill you. I won't rest until I find the person responsible."

"It's not Trey," MJ snapped stopping in the middle of the parking lot.

"You don't know that."

"I *do*," she yelled. "He's sick!"

Her eyes widened and she bit her lip. "Pretend I didn't say that."

She panned the area. "I hope nobody overheard me."

MJ turned her attention to him. "Damn it, Mike. No one in the industry knows. You can't tell anyone."

"Calm down. I won't. But you have to explain." He looked around for a place they could talk privately and settled on a bench away from the sound stages. "Sit for a minute."

"I don't have time for this," she balked.

Mike patted the seat next to him. "Do all you Hollywood types give me shit? Sit, Mary Jean."

Giving him an eye roll, she sat down heavily beside him.

"You have to promise me to keep what I tell you to yourself."

"You have my word."

"After I came home from Valselo, Trey asked me to come to his office. I was bogged down with preproduction, and it was late when I finally made it there. Everyone had left for the day, but his light was still on, so I let myself in. I overheard him on the phone. I don't know who he was talking to, most likely Nicole. He said the doctor called and his suspicions were confirmed. It's Parkinson's. Then he started to cry. I didn't know what to do so I sat down in the waiting room until I heard him finish the call." She took a deep breath. "I went into his office and admitted that I had heard his diagnosis."

"How did he react?"

"He asked me to please keep it to myself. I promised him I wouldn't tell anyone, and I offered to help him any way I could. Then he told me the reason that he had requested the meeting. He asked me to codirect and produce his next film. He seemed relieved that I knew the truth, and he didn't have to hide it from me." She rose from the bench and looked down at Mike. "Trey is not a killer. I have to go work."

Mike stayed put and watched MJ until she safely entered the guarded door of the sound stage. Amy was already asleep when he gently edged into the bed next to her. He spent the night staring at the ceiling. He disagreed with MJ. Trey was still his number one suspect. He just had to figure out what the guy had to gain if he eliminated his sister.

Credit for her film? Maybe. One thing for sure. Trey struck Mike as completely remorseless.

Chapter 23

Amy luxuriated on a chaise lounge in the shade of her deck's awning. The ceiling fan overhead stirred a refreshing breeze. She squinted at the ocean vista far below; the blue-green waves topped with blinding sun sparkle diamonds beneath a cloudless blue sky. Two weeks after the filming of *Rose of the Adriatic* had wrapped, Amy still hadn't relaxed her way out of the tension and anxiety that working on MJ's set had involved. No amount of mindless lazing by the pool could stop her from worrying about her sister of the heart.

MJ hardly slept, and if she did, it was frequently on the sofa in her office at the studio. During her rare breaks from toiling in the editing room, MJ gobbled down meals that Amy lovingly prepared for her and Mike, took long drenching showers and collapsed in bed no later than eight PM. She was up and out long before Amy awoke each day.

That MJ worked herself into exhaustion didn't overly concern Amy. She knew how driven to succeed with her first production MJ was and how much that success would mean for MJ's career – and hers and Brian's careers, also. What worried Amy constantly was the fact that the security guards who had provided comforting assurance to the cast and crew after the car explosion no longer manned their posts. MJ's office and the editing room weren't secure at all other than a couple of guards in the lobby and at the entry gates. The killer had gotten through those gates before.

Mike had assumed the role of a one-man security team as much as the murder investigation and his sister's obstinacy would permit. MJ couldn't deal with the loss of her assistant, especially since the murderer had missed the mark killing an unintended victim instead of her. She had asked Jody to fetch her script from the car. The guilt gnawed at MJ incessantly. Her grief manifested as thorniness. The anger fueled her desire to make the movie perfect to somehow make the tragedy seem worth it, and she single-mindedly drove herself to that end regardless that the killer was still at large, and Mike kept telling her that she was in danger.

Amy sighed and took a sip of water that had gone warm during the eighty-degree afternoon. She swung her legs off the chaise and rose to her feet. The stone pavers had super-heated in the sun. Amy skip-hopped, the bottoms of her feet burning, to the edge of the pool and dove in. The heated water still jarred her hot skin and goosebumps rose along her arms and legs. Three freestyle strokes later her body had regulated to the temperature and the invigorating zing of the swim.

She was breast stroking underwater when the surface above her erupted in ripples. Mike torpedoed beneath her, rolled over and flashed her a smile. Amy surfaced treading water. He shot out of the water in front of her like a breeching whale. She turned her head amid the splashing and roll of his wake. His arms corralled her. He pressed her against his chest, and she wrapped her legs around his waist.

The water was up to his shoulders. Mike carried her

to the edge of the pool as she leaned back her head into the water trailing floating tendrils of her raven hair feeling weightless and free. She gripped the ladder rungs, got a foothold on the lowest step, and climbed out of the water while Mike playfully gave her two "helping hands" under her bottom. Laughing, she retrieved a towel from the patio table, wrapped it over her shoulders and threw a fresh towel to Mike when he emerged from the pool.

He padded over to the table, water dripping off his swim trunks and muscled body. A thrill ran through her knowing every inch of that gorgeous man intimately. Gratitude and wonder ballooned inside her that Mike was hers and she was his.

She sensed that the movie would not only succeed, it would triumph. Anna's story documented the miraculous. How could the movie about her life not astonish the audiences? If she were right about the movie's box office popularity, Amy, Brian, and MJ could pick their projects *and* their locations. Maybe Amy might have her forever with Mike at last and still nurture the career that she loved.

An idea sparked in Amy's mind. MJ might be interested in renting Amy's house for just enough money to cover her overhead. Amy *could* move back to Chicago. Her next project for the Hallmark Channel was due to start filming in a month in Canada. Chicago wasn't that much farther from British Columbia than Los Angeles.

Besides, an additional location shoot was scheduled in North Carolina in a charming little Christmas town. She'd be much closer to that site with Chicago as a home base. The more she thought about the plan, the more appeal it held. Even if MJ wasn't interested in renting her house, Amy was certain that she could sell easily, and probably make a profit.

After she previewed the movie, assuming when the final credits rolled that she'd deem it good enough for a healthy box office draw, Amy would call her agent, talk to MJ and put the plan in motion.

She gazed at Mike bursting to tell him what she was considering, but she held back. Better to put eveything in place and surprise him.

"Are you done working for the day?" Amy said tucking her towel around her sarong style.

"Yep." He scrubbed his close cropped, black hair with the towel and then hung it over the back of a chair.

"Oh good. I'm making pasta with artichokes, capers, cherry tomatoes, and olives for dinner. Did you see MJ at all today?"

"I did. She actually smiled at me. I hardly recognized her."

Amy burst out laughing. "I'm *real* interested in what you did to make her smile because I have totally failed no matter what I've done the past couple weeks."

"Didn't do a thing. She finished work on the movie. She's happy about that, I think."

"That's fantastic. Do you think she'll be home soon?"

"Yes, she said she'd be here in time for dinner."

"I hope we three can celebrate tonight. I'll start cooking after I shower the chlorine off."

"Sounds great, especially the shower part. I need to get all this chlorine off, too." He winked and gave her an impish smile.

She clasped his hand in response and towed him

inside.

MJ's disposition had radically improved from the minute she walked through the door and bounded upstairs to join Amy and Mike in the kitchen. She was sunny and jokey and back to teasing her brother rather than battling with him. She tackled the food on her plate with gusto and took a second helping.

"This is so delicious, Amy. Thank you." She shoveled a heap of pasta onto her fork.

"Of course. You're welcome. Glad you like it." Amy sat back in her chair and took a sip of wine happy to watch MJ eating a meal with enjoyment.

"Mike said you finished the movie today," Amy said.

"I did and I'm thrilled with it." MJ picked up her empty plate, stacked Mike's and Amy's plates atop hers and carried them to the sink.

MJ opened the dishwasher and turned on the faucet. Rinsing and loading the dishes, she said, "The final cut is ready for the execs to view and approve for distribution. In our case, that's Nicole and her dad's rubber stamp."

Amy brought her empty wine glass over to the dishwasher. "I'm so excited, MJ. Do I get to see it soon?"

"Hell, yeah. I want you there when I preview it for Nicole. Brian, too. I haven't heard back from her, but tentatively the screening is set for tomorrow afternoon at two o'clock."

"Oh, wow! I can't wait. Where do I go on the movie lot?"

"There are several projection rooms in the main office building. We'll drive to the lot together, and I'll take you to the room. Brian will meet us. He's worked in the other productions there before and knows his way around."

"Can Mike come, too?"

"Uh…" MJ faltered. "I don't think I can swing that…"

"No worries, sis. I've got appointments all day tomorrow. Sam Martinez and I are meeting first thing in the morning and working the case all day."

"Working the case." MJ shivered. "Gives me the creeps thinking that I'm a case."

Mike rolled his eyes. "You've always been a case," he teased. "Gives me the creeps that you've been alone, sometimes all night in that place."

MJ waved a hand in dismissal. "No worries. I'm a Sullivan-Lynch. I can take care of myself."

"Yeah right." Mike wagged his head. "Martinez and I can't catch a break in this case. Every interview leads nowhere. The hottest suspect is still Trey Ross, but he's more lukewarm the harder we look at him. I'm focused on him largely because he's a combative jerk."

"You're absolutely right," MJ said on a laugh. "But as I've told you, he'd never hurt me, no less end my life."

She hung her head. "Or my Jody's, either."

Tears welled in MJ's eyes and Amy drew her into her arms. For the first time during the long weeks of trouble on her set, MJ broke down and sobbed, her shoulders heaving. Amy gazed at Mike frowning as MJ finally released her pent-up emotion. Mike's somber expression and the fire in his eyes told Amy that nothing would stop his solving the case.

Amy knew that his heart was breaking for his sister when he said with a chipper tone, "How about we watch that Edward and Jacob duke it out in the Twilight Saga?"

MJ lifted her head off Amy's shoulder and hooted a laugh. "Whoa. Who are you and what have you done with my sarcastic, unromantic brother?"

Mike knit his brow. "*Unromantic*? I beg to differ. Tell her, Ames."

Amy burst out laughing. "You're very romantic, Michael. Remember the lily of the valley and the florist shop of roses you gave me?"

"Damn straight. Did you hear that, Mary Jean? Not to mention how romantic I am in the bedroom."

"Oh, *please*." MJ covered her ears. "TMI."

A wicked grin bloomed on Mike's face. "I've got the moves, don't I, Ames? How many times did we…"

MJ shut her brother up by slugging his arm. "Stop it!"

Mike guffawed, as always, delighted to torment his kid sister.

"Are you done?" MJ said.

"Not really…"

MJ made a fist and pulled back her arm threatening to land another punch.

"Enough," Amy admonished beaming at him.

He gave her a wink, his cheeks dimpling with his Cheshire grin. "Case closed. I'm *very* romantic."

"Geesh," MJ said. "Just for toying with me, we're going to binge watch all *four* Twilight movies. *And* the behind-the-scenes footage, too."

"Shoot me now," Mike said. He drifted to the sectional and plopped down in the middle seat patting the cushions on either side of him. "Bring it on, Mary Jean. The sooner we start, the sooner we finish."

Giggling, the women joined him.

He turned his head to face MJ. "Anyway, I'm

betting that you fall asleep in say, ten minutes and I'm home free."

She punched his arm in response and picked up the remote control queuing up *Twilight*.

Mike was off on his prediction. MJ fell asleep in five minutes, her head thrown back against the leather cushion, her mouth hanging open and emitting purring snores.

"I'd holler I told you so," he whispered in Amy's ear. "But that would wake her up and I'd have to watch more of this dreck."

His warm breath in her ear brought a rush of attraction and a tightening in her core. She was endlessly drawn to him, always wanting more.

Amy needed justice for Jody's death and the attempts to take MJ's life; and she knew that Mike would identify the criminal and make him pay. But when he did, he'd leave California and go back to his career with the CPD.

Mike had spoiled Amy living with her for weeks while they both worked the jobs that they loved. That could be her life every day…and night. She had no desire to return to long distance loving the man of her dreams. Would he embrace her plan to move? She'd want to move into his condo with him. Was he ready for that big step in their relationship?

Her heart told her, yes. She'd talk with her agent and MJ in the morning.

He gently lifted MJ into his arms as if she were weightless. She didn't so much as flutter her closed eyelids, she was so deep asleep. Amy scooped the remote control off the coffee table and powered off the TV.

"I'll get the lights," she said softly.

He nodded and whisked his sister away. Amy switched off the lights on the upper floor closing the blinds as she went room to room. Then she bounded downstairs to her bedroom, eager for Mike to display his romantic nature.

Chapter 24

Mike and Sam Martinez huddled over the detective's cluttered desk cross-referencing the Studio's security log entries with the dates that the accidents and car bombing had happened. It was no surprise that Trey Ross had entered through the gates driving different cars on the dates in question.

Trey had free access and opportunity. But no motive that Mike could determine coupled with his sister's vehement denials that her former boss was guilty.

"Nothing's jumping out at me," Mike said rubbing his eyes. "But we're missing something here and I'll be damned if I can piece it together."

"Yeah." Martinez leaned back in his chair.

"Wait a minute," Mike said. "Could you check the entries again? Who was on duty at the gate during those dates?"

Martinez nodded and bent to the task. "Let's see," he picked up the log and thumbed through it. "Don't know if it's useful but the same guard was at the main gate on all four dates. His name is Harold Teller. Hang on."

Sam picked up the handset on his desk phone and dialed a number. "Hello Jim. Sam Martinez LAPD. Good. And you? Good to hear. Listen, can you check your schedule and tell me the next time Harold Teller is at the gate?"

Mike waited for the response.

"Good," Sam said. "Thanks. You, too."

He hung up the phone. "He's on the afternoon shift. Comes in at 1:30."

"I'll talk with him. Maybe he'll remember something more helpful about the comings and goings through his checkpoint. Can I take the logbook with me?"

"Sure. I still want to hang on to it just in case it magically proves useful."

"No problem. I'll bring it back after I speak with him."

"See you later."

Mike itched to tug on this slim investigative thread. But he had a couple hours to kill before the meeting with the guard. He placed a few blue tooth calls to remaining women on the list who had left Ross productions because they supposedly came on to the "happily married" director as he drove back to Amy's house, with the same straight to voicemail results.

When he entered the gate code and pulled up to the garage apron, he discovered that MJ's car was gone. He used the house key Amy had given him to enter the front door. "Hello," he called out.

No answer.

He went straight into Amy's bedroom inhaling a lungful of her unique scent that perfumed the air. Mike changed into swim trunks deep in thought. Ah, the California lifestyle. He was getting too used to sun saturated days. Chicago's overshadowing gray weather and gloom dampened the prospect of homecoming a lot. Not to mention how impossible living the bachelor life appeared to him now that he'd lived as a couple with the woman he loved.

Mike had enjoyed working with Sam. Could he pull off a transfer to the LAPD? He had no idea how to go about that but felt sure his law enforcement steeped family could help. But is that what he really wanted?

With a shake of his head, he left the bedroom and made his way through the house out to the pool. His career, his "village" in the Midwest meant everything. He had never considered moving away. Mike loved the city on Lake Michigan – the food, the people, the lifestyle – way more than he liked LA. True, the weather back home sucked most of the time, but family, friendships, cozy fireplaces and blessed air conditioning made up for the tundra cold, gloom and blazing temperatures with high humidity during the largely two seasons of the year. Amy had the Midwest in her bones, too. They'd make it work somehow. Outside he dove into the pool glad that his respite in LaLa land hadn't ended yet.

****

Refreshed and loose-limbed, Mike got behind the wheel of the car and traveled through sluggish traffic to the massive Studio entrance. He drove through the lane on the right side of the guardhouse and rolled down his window displaying his badge.

"Afternoon," he said. "I need to speak with Harold Teller when he checks in. Can I park over there," he pointed to the left, "and come inside?"

"Sure." The guard handed a placard through the window. "Just put this on the dash."

Mike parked the car and sauntered to the guardhouse carrying the logbook. He went inside, shook the guard's hand, and accepted a seat on a swivel chair the guard rolled toward him at a desk height counter running the length of the building in front of windows facing the street.

"Harry should be here any minute. He's usually early to his shifts. Lives for the job. You'll see when you meet him," Jim said.

"Thanks."

Harry arrived minutes later as predicted. He waved to the guardhouse as he drove past triggering the gate to open remotely. When he appeared in the guardhouse's door, Mike marveled that the guy could even walk. Harry was largely bald with a fringe of snow colored hair circling his head an inch or so above his ears. He hunched over as he moved stoop shouldered, and his uniform hung loose on his bony frame. Mike gauged his age about twenty years past retirement.

"Hey Jim," Harry said. "And who might you be, sir?"

Mike rose from his seat accepting a handshake from the geezer. "Mike Lynch. I'm a homicide detective with the Chicago police on assignment with the LAPD investigating the car bombing here."

"I see." Harry put a large thermos down on the desk in front of Jim. "Have a nice evening with your family, Jim."

"Sure thing, Harry." Jim rose and Harry eased into his vacant chair. "See ya."

"So, what can I do for you, Detective Lynch?"

"I'd like to go over the visitor log with you, specifically on four dates you were on duty."

"Of course. Shoot."

Mike opened the log and set it on the desk in front of Harry. He read off the dates he wanted to focus on,

215

and Harry recited the entries squinting through bottle-bottomed eyeglasses – painstakingly slowly.

"Can you please look one more time at Trey Ross's visits? Anything unusual that you recall? Any detail, no matter how insignificant with respect to other visitors might help, too."

Harry leaned back heavily in his chair. "You know I've been on the job since Hollywood City Studios opened. Mr. Swann treats me like family, and he trusts me to keep this place safe. There has *never* been a reason for homicide detectives to pay me a visit. No less several visits. Everything is right there in the log. And when Miss Nicole told me to shut the gate down, it was done. Period."

"Mr. Swann?"

"The founder. Great man."

"Ah." Mike nodded, frustrated with the dead lead. He slid the open log back towards him along the countertop and glanced at it again.

"Hold it…" he said, his pulse accelerating. "There are several entries on these dates where you noted passengers in the vehicles. How come that's not the case with Trey Ross? I know for sure he was with his wife Nicole on at least two of the dates I'm looking into."

"It's not down there because they never come here together."

"Well, they were definitely on the grounds together." Mike scrutinized the log again. "Why isn't she logged in anywhere?"

Harry patted his shirt pocket. "Because her visits are right here in a private log."

"Private? Let me see it."

The guard slipped a slim date calendar out of his

pocket and handed it over.

Mike leafed through it until he reached the first date in question. There was the entry – Miss Nicole, at five thirty AM. "I don't get it. Why do you keep two logs?"

"Always have for the Swann family. Per the boss's express orders. They never stop at the gate, of course. We just wave them through. Even Miss Nicole when she was just a little thing. She'd whiz by on her bike most days. She practically lived here summers and most days after school, too. I remember she was always so interested in big action sequences on the sets. She hung around with the special effects crew all the time. Smart little thing."

The cogs fell into place for Mike. "Did she come in today?"

"You'd have to ask Jim. As you can see, I just got here."

"Call him. He keeps a private log too, right?"

"Yep." Harry slowly, very slowly, too slowly accomplished the call as Mike's heartbeat drummed in his ears.

"Hey Jim. Miss Nicole here today?" He tilted his head and squinted out the window. "Got it. Thanks."

"She's here now. Came in at 10:30 AM today."

Mike sprang to his feet and was halfway out the door calling over his shoulder, "Which building?"

"Don't know," Harry boomed. "Probably main office."

"Thanks, Harry." Mike sprinted to the car, whipped open the door, leaned inside and grabbed the radio transmitter off the console. "Patch me through to Sam Martinez," he barked.

He flung himself into the car, ignited the engine and

screeched out of the parking slot. "Martinez here. Lynch?"

"Yeah, Sam. How far are you from Hollywood City Studios?"

"Twenty with traffic. Why?"

"Make it in ten, Code three. We've been looking at the wrong Ross. Nicole Ross is here. Head to the main office. I'm going to try to find her now. I'll let you know if she's elsewhere. Fast, Sam. MJ and Amy are here, too. Meeting with Nicole."

****

"That was so much fun," Amy said spinning in the chair behind MJ's desk. "When was the last time we went shopping for nothing together?"

MJ grinned. "Gosh, I can't remember. We really should rename our sprees…when we shop for nothing, we can hardly fit all our loot in the car!"

Amy burst out laughing. MJ came up behind her and tapped on her computer keyboard awakening the display. "Oh good. Nicole accepted the meeting invitation," she said. "We're on with viewing the Final Cut at two. We have fifteen minutes. Let's go the screening room. Are you hungry?"

"No, I'm good. I can't wait to see the movie."

A broad smile lit MJ's face and her green eyes glimmered. "I can't wait for you to see it. You'll be proud."

"I hope so. No regrets at taking a chance with me?"

"Are you kidding? Bethany Chambers can't hold your coat. Her quitting was the best thing that could have happened to this project."

"Aw, thanks sweetie."

Amy shoved back the desk chair and stood. She dug

in her purse for her cell phone.

"Let's leave our phones here, OK?" MJ said. "I don't want any distractions during the screening."

"Good idea." She stowed her phone and then slipped her purse into MJ's desk drawer.

Linking arms with MJ, Amy traipsed down winding hallways in the huge building until they reached Screening Room Seven. The mini auditorium held four rows of stadium cushy, recliner seating facing the screen. A beam of white light, dust mote sparkles dancing, arrowed from the projection room pooling on the screen. Amy sat down and crossed her legs, waiting for the show to begin and daydreaming about how she could make the most of her free time between her upcoming project…and future work, too, with Mike.

MJ paced in the rear of the auditorium, mumbling.

"Come sit down, MJ."

"I can't sit. I'm too antsy. Where the heck is Nicole anyway? It's not like her to be late."

"What time is it?"

"It's…Oh crap. I left my phone back in my office."

"Yes, I know." Amy patted the arm of the chair next to her. "Come sit anyway, MJ. I'm sure she'll be here soon. What about Brian?"

"Good question." MJ perched on the edge of the seat next to Amy. "We can start when Nicole gets here, Brian or no Brian."

"OK. I wouldn't want him to miss it, though. Want me to run back to your office and give him a call?"

"Nah. Then you might miss the opening scene. We'll just have to wait for—"

A loud click from behind them had Amy and MJ whipping their heads around.

"What was that?" Amy said.

"Definitely the door." MJ jumped out of her seat and lunged up the steps to the rear of the auditorium. She pushed down on the door handle and then tugged it hard. "It's locked from the outside. What the hell?"

MJ kept tugging at the handle while Amy rushed to help her. Together they began banging on the door and shouting out their predicament, hopeful to catch somebody's attention.

Minutes passed and no assistance materialized. MJ walked in front of the projected beam. "Hello? Anybody there?"

No answer.

Amy's nose stung and her eyes burned. She swore she smelled smoke. A loud pop sounded. Turning toward the sound coming from the front of the room, she froze. The edges of the screen were blackening and turning to soot smoldering and rapidly curling from the outside edges to the center.

"MJ, look! The screen's on fire!"

"Oh my god." MJ rushed to the far wall toward the fire extinguisher box. The box opened, but the extinguisher was missing.

Gray black plumes of thick smoke rolled from the "stage" area up the aisles. Coughing, MJ and Amy banged their fists on the door.

"Help! Fire! Someone! Help!"

Amy's lungs filled with searing fumes. Every breath felt like a knife stab. She teetered on her feet, her mind scrambling to figure out some way for them to escape. MJ staggered back to the projection opening. "Are you in there?" she screamed.

A female cackled.

"Who's there?"

Silence.

Amy dropped to the floor the carpet musty under her face. The air was slightly clearer, and she shouted, "MJ. Get down low. You can breathe a little better."

The smoke kept churning, obscuring everything around Amy. She closed her stinging eyes and drifted away envisioning the view from Mike's sky house condo in Chicago. Like in the City, she heard the wail of a siren.

Chapter 25

Mike barreled into the foyer holding his shield out in his hand. "Where are the projection rooms?" he bellowed at two security guards behind the reception desk.

"Calm down, fella," a salt and pepper haired, paunchy, pasty guy said in a bored tone.

"Homicide department emergency, *fella*," Mike spat out. "What room or rooms are being used today? Quick."

"Uh," the guy said turning his attention to a paper on his desk. "Looks like seven and ten."

"Where?"

"Top floor. There are signs."

He raced to the elevator and pushed the call button. "Do you know the room assignments? Mary Jean Lynch, specifically?"

"Seven."

The elevator's doors glided open, and Mike rushed inside the car. On the ride up he transmitted the room location to Sam whose ETA was five minutes. He sped the corridors' twists and turns while his gut told him that he had to move faster, ever faster. When he detected the smell of smoke getting stronger as he drew closer to the screening room, his adrenaline surged.

Panting, he called the fire in to the LACFD adding that he suspected people were trapped in screening room seven. The sound of Martinez's wailing siren approaching brought a smidgeon of encouragement. Mike reached the projection room door dismayed at the river of smoke underneath it, creeping sinister tendrils along the floorboards. He grabbed the door handle and yanked his hand away sharply, his palm instantly blistering.

Mike stripped off his suit jacket and wrapped some of the material around his hand. He grabbed the handle again and shoved against the door with his shoulder, hardly budging it. "Amy, MJ!" he screamed. "Can you hear me?"

The silence in response had him frantically searching for something to break the door lock. Heavy footfalls sounded from down the hallway – boots on the run. A fire squad in full gear advanced toward him. He cleared away from the door allowing the lead man to wield a Halligan bar making quit work disengaging the cylinder lock busting the doors wide open. Smoke disgorged from the room in evil black clouds. The squad swarmed to the front of the room to deal with the active flames.

"Here," a firefighter said, handing Mike a small oxygen tank and mask. "Gear up. Come on."

He put on the mask, triggered oxygen flow from the tank and propelled into the room behind the fireman. Amy and MJ lay side by side, face down on the floor.

His informal partner pantomimed directions. Mike raced to Amy, and the firefighter sped to MJ. They hoisted the women over their shoulders and carried them out into the hallway placing them on their backs on the floor a good distance from the billowing smoke.

Mike dropped to his knees and gently pressed his ear against Amy's chest. Maybe just the faintest air flow. He pressed his finger against her neck and then blew out his held breath when he detected a faint pulse. Gratitude that he wasn't too late streamed through him like a balm. The fire squad man straddled MJ, and Mike straddled Amy administering CPR.

Martinez burst through the doorway.

"We've got this," Mike said. "Find Nicole Ross. She's got to be here somewhere."

Sam spun around and sped away.

Amy's eyelids fluttered and then she heaved sputtering. Mike enfolded her in his arms, rocking, offering silent prayers of thanksgiving. MJ came to gagging and coughing.

"It's OK," he soothed. "I've got you, Ames. It's OK. I'm here. I love you. I've got you."

Her eyes streamed tears. Four EMT's brought two stretchers down the hall and gently pried Amy from Mike's arms to attend to her. MJ was hoisted onto a stretcher in similar condition.

Mike stood on shaky legs and clasped Amy's hand. Her angelic smile through the oxygen mask lit his soul. "Are you taking her to the hospital?"

"I'll check her out at the truck first, but I'm leaning towards yes."

"Can I ride with her?"

"Sure thing."

He walked awkwardly alongside the gurney refusing to let her hand go for even a second. Her eyes were closed but her chest rose and fell softly, a beautiful sight.

The stretcher was rolled onto the truck and Mike climbed inside, ducked down and crouch-walked to sit on the horizontal bench. He took Amy's hand in his and held it gently.

She pulled the oxygen mask down to her chin. "I love you," she whispered. "Thank you so much. How did you know we were in trouble?"

He smiled and gently put the mask in place. "Hey, what can I say? I *am* a detective you know."

Her grin and dancing eyes assured him that she'd be OK. "We'll talk after they take care of you at the hospital. Rest for now."

One of the doors swung shut. Before the second door was secured Mike caught sight of Martinez half-shoving Nicole Ross into his squad car.

At the ER, Amy and MJ received immediate attention and hours of monitoring. Sometime after dusk fell, Ryder came careening into Amy's room. Mike hardly recognized the celebrity with his mussed hair and creased clothes. "Where is she?" he blurted out.

"Next door," Mike said.

Ryder turned tail and dashed away.

Mike chuckled. "Pretty sure MJ has a ride home."

"Yep. Seems so. Do we?"

He realized that he had left the car at the Studio. "If we hitch with them, we do."

A nurse supplied discharge instructions and released Amy to Mike's care. Ryder shepherded MJ. The couples walked out of the hospital into the soft, balmy night. MJ and Ryder climbed into the front seat of the rental car that he had parked askew near the ER entrance. Mike helped Amy into the backseat, skirted the rear of the car and got in beside her. He gathered her against his side, and she lay her head on his shoulder. During the brief ride to retrieve the car, Mike savored her sweet closeness.

After they switched cars, Amy and Mike stopped at an In and Out Burger restaurant on the way home. The fresh from the grill smell of cheeseburgers and fries filled the car. Martinez checked in with Mike when they were halfway home.

"She's in custody and screaming like a banshee," he said without preamble when Mike connected the call.

"Good. What's she screaming? How dare you? Do you know how important I am? That kind of thing?"

"Nah, surprisingly. She's totally unhinged and rambling something about that bitch, MJ will never keep her mouth shut about Trey's secret. She's screamed more than once that MJ will ruin us, she doesn't deserve to live, and I won't give up until I shut her up permanently."

"I know something about that secret she's unhinged about. Hopefully the threats and roundabout admission will make it easy to nail her despite her money and influence."

"You up for gathering evidence with me tomorrow? I've locked down the scene."

"Of course. See you in the morning."

"Nice work, Lynch."

"You too, Martinez."

****

Under the stars nestled in a chaise lounge on Amy's terrace after scarfing down the takeout food, Mike softly kissed the crown of Amy's head tenderly warming her.

She arched her neck and gazed at his handsome face shadowed in the moonlight. "I can't believe Nicole is a murderer," she said.

"Don't think about any of this. I'll meet Sam tomorrow to make sure the case against her is airtight. How are you feeling?"

"A little wobbly." She kissed the side of his neck. "And I'm dreading your leaving. I can't stand thinking about not being with you at the end of every day."

"I feel the same way. But nothing has changed. If anything, I love you more than when we first agreed to stay together long distance. Who knows? Maybe I can wrangle more special assignments with the LAPD. Sam's a great partner. And I think the feeling is mutual."

She nodded her head. "Maybe I have a better solution."

"Oh yeah, What's that?"

"Take me home, Mike."

"You are home, Ames."

"I mean home home."

He sat erect. "Are you serious? You'd leave California for me?"

"Uh huh. I've already made some tentative arrangements. MJ might want to rent this house – even buy it if her career takes off like I think it will. That's if the movie is green-lighted now that Nicole is heading to prison. What a mess."

"Don't worry. Trey will make sure the movie's a go."

"You're probably right. I hope."

"Let's get back to your leaving California. Nothing would make me happier, Ames."

"Really?" She gazed up into his shimmering eyes. "I love you so much, Mike. I know I can't be happy unless we're together."

"I've had a crush on you since you came to my house on Thanksgiving Day when you were ten."

She arched her eyebrows. "You're kidding! Why did you never tell me that before?"

"Because…" he said pulling her closer to his chest. "I've never proposed to you before. I've loved you since the first moment I met you and I will love you forever. Will you marry me?"

Amy threw her arms around his neck, tears welling. "Ditto," she said. "And yes."

Epilogue

Amy paced in front of the floor to ceiling windows. She balled her fist and kneaded her aching lower back. Bending at the waist, she reached her fingertips towards her toes attempting to touch them with the deep stretch. Who was she kidding?

She hooted a laugh. Amy hadn't seen her feet in months.

"Mike, where are you?" Her voice echoed in the high-ceilinged condo. Was one of those cars whizzing down below on the LaSalle Street bridge Mike's?

Entertainment Tonight was muted on the television. The red carpet preshow in progress made Amy even more impatient for Mike's arrival. He had promised her that he would come home in time to watch with her.

Her phone vibrated and skittered along the kitchen counter. She lumbered at top speed, for her, to answer before voicemail kicked in.

"I'm here, Honey, just parking the car, I'll be up in a minute," he said without a single pause or taking a breath.

She smiled at his unspoken apology. "Thanks, love. Hurry up."

Amy waddled over to the couch and plopped down. The coffee table in front of her was set for the big night, only lacking the Lou Malnati's pizza and cheddar cubes that Mike had just picked up at the Wells Street restaurant.

Mike rammed through the door, set the pizza carton and bag down on the coffee table and leaned in to kiss Amy's lips – a long, delicious, Mike-style kiss. "I missed you," he said.

"Aw…" she brushed a hand on his cheek tenderly.

"Thank you for all this." She waved her hand over the coffee table.

"Of course. It's your special night…"

"Oh my god! There she is." Tears welled as Amy grabbed the remote and raised the volume. "Doesn't she look *beautiful*? And look at Ry. So handsome. They make such an adorable couple."

She gaped at the screen in amazement observing MJ calmly chat with Kevin Frazier as if she spoke with famous talk show hosts on camera every day.

"If it's all right with you, Kevin, may I say hello to Amy Jordan Sullivan watching from home?"

He gave her a nod.

"Hi Amy," MJ's eyes sparkled looking directly into the camera. "I wish you could be here tonight. But I'll gladly accept your award when your name is called."

Beaming, seemingly right at Amy, she touched the dainty bracelet on her wrist and winked. "Thank you, Kevin."

"You are welcome. Good luck, Amy," he said into the camera.

Turning his attention back to MJ standing next to him resplendent in her shimmering gown and dripping with loaned diamonds, he said, "And best of luck to you, too, MJ."

MJ swept away down the red carpet toward the Dolby Theater.

"I can't believe that your sister just gave me a shout-out on national TV. And she's wearing the bracelet I sent to her." Amy held out her wrist displaying her matching bracelet.

Last month after the Academy Awards nominations were announced, Amy contacted Anna requesting that she send the bracelets from Valselo, simply asking that whatever she chose should be handmade there in the village.

Anna had sent her a lovely choice of strung wooden beads carved into delicate roses which delighted Amy. What better way to bless the nominees and the movie? Amy had received the Best Actress nomination, MJ was nominated for Best Director, Brian for Best Supporting Actor and *Rose of the Adriatic* was up for Best Picture.

Amy went to use the washroom at a commercial break while Mike set out their meal.

"Mike, could you please come here?" she hollered from the bathroom. "My water just broke!"

Contractions started almost immediately.

"Whoa," Amy said leaning against the sink. "We better get to the hospital."

Mike grabbed Amy's packed bag and crooked an elbow so that she could lean on his arm making her way to the elevator. Amy slouched in the passenger seat, breathing, and panting through wave upon wave of contractions, much relieved when Mike screeched to a halt and raced around the front bumper to help her into a wheelchair at Chicago Regional Hospital. For half the ride Amy was afraid she'd deliver in the car.

Molly met them at the door and had Amy whisked up to the Maternity Floor. After less than a half hour pushing, Amy sat propped in bed with her baby snuggled against her chest and her husband by her side.

Mike tuned the television to the all-important broadcast in progress with uncanny perfect timing.

"The Oscar for Best Actress in a Leading Role goes to…" Then came the tense pause while the year's prior Best Actor winner, Brock Cuchna, opened the envelope. "Amy Jordan Sullivan."

Amy clapped a hand over her mouth hugging the baby even closer.

Mike enveloped her in a broad hug while each of them kept an eye trained on the screen.

MJ walked gracefully up the stairs, accepted the golden statuette, and took her place at the mic. "When we were little kids, Amy and I dreamed of standing on this stage one day. We even practiced our acceptance speeches mugging in the mirror. Amy, I wish you were here right now. Our dreams have come true."

She raised the award in her right hand. "But Amy is not here tonight for the best reason. Amy and my brother, Mike, are celebrating the birth of a little boy just fifteen minutes ago. May I be the first to welcome my nephew. Welcome to the world Oscar Sullivan Lynch!"

A word about the author…

K.M. Daughters is the penname for team writers and sisters, Pat Casiello and Kathie Clare. The penname is dedicated to the memory of their parents, "K"ay and "M"ickey Lynch. K.M. Daughters is the author of 17 award winning romance genre novels. The "Daughters" are wives, mothers and grandmothers residing in the Chicago suburbs and on the Outer Banks, North Carolina. Visitors are most welcome at www.kmdaughters.com